DREAMS OF GOLD

Jonathan Chamberlain

Long Island Press

FT
Pbk

Published in Great Britain by
Long Island Press

A CIP catalogue record for this book
is available from the British Library.

ISBN 978-0-9545960-4-0

The author may be contacted at
www.longislandpress.co.uk

*For Patrick and Christie and to
the loving memory of Stevie*

Part One

1.

The carp in the pool swirled in a sudden frenzy for the crumbs of dried bread that the man scattered over the surface. He watched them tumble and slither over each other as they battled desperately for the little parcels of food.

'Perhaps, that is how it is with us,' thought the man. 'The gods scatter fairy dust and we swirl and tumble in a desperate desire to grab it. To the winner, the spoils. To him who comes second, nothing.' He sighed. 'Truly, it is a cruel world. The creation of cruel Gods.'

The bread was quickly gone but the surface of the pond still rippled with activity.

'We care not for the next man.' He shook his head slowly as if weighed down by the heavy burden of his thoughts. The ways of the world were not his ways. He was a poet. Poets did not swirl with the rest of personkind. Poets did not swim with other fish, did not share the need for earthly goodies. Poets could go hungry if need be. Which reminded him. It must be about lunchtime. He wondered what little goodie his dear Bronwyn had prepared. He looked down events to organize, the national teams to accommodate, the medals to design, the tickets to print and distribute and all the rest of it. Mountains of detail. Above all there was the Opening Ceremony to arrange. And each of these details had to be budgeted for. The money had to be raised. The money that had been raised needed to be carefully handled—invested when not needed; disbursed with a clearly demarcated paper trail when required. And he, Lord Coe, was responsible for making sure this entire edifice of planning and effort worked. And now they were almost there. Eight hard years. He looked from face to face to see who was looking relaxed and who was still looking stressed. Eight damned hard years. But as he knew from his years as an athlete, all the hard work was aimed at one short moment, one perfect explosion of effort— and the result was either glory or mud in the face. And you didn't know till that last moment which it would be. And now there was this Tibetan demonstration. It might just be a flea bite or ... he hardly dare say it, even to himself, it could turn this moment of dreams into a nightmare. It wasn't in his nature to let things slide. He wanted things taken in hand. Every single minutia.

Finally he sat down. The firm set of his jaw alerted everyone that there was not going to be champagne. Not just yet. That would come later. Lord Coe let his gaze circle the table slowly so that each one of them would be left in no doubt as to the seriousness with which he viewed the matter.

'Today demonstrations by Tibetans. Tomorrow ...?' He left the thought dangling in the silence of the room. What outrage might there be? From the very beginning, careful thought had been given to the security issues. He spoke forcefully: 'There is a danger that events could get out of hand. We have to seize the initiative. We have to take charge of the idea. We have to capture the moral high ground. The question is: How? How are we to do this?' He needed answers. One by one, eyes turned away from his steely glare: to the table, the far wall, the ceiling. Coming up with instant ideas was not what they were good at. They were used to delegating. Everything was delegated. Now he wanted them—them?—to come up with an idea. Was he mad?

Only one pair of eyes did not seek to escape. Mary Smith, Head of Strategy, had not got where she was without one or two ideas of her own. In fact, she had a file of ideas for every possible emergency. She had already worked out six years earlier that there would be a requirement for an idea— she didn't know when, where, by who, in what circumstance, in what context—but she knew that it was one hundred percent certain that the request would come. So she had drafted a short list of five ideas for every contingency she could think of. Well, truth was, she had got her smart team to come up with the ideas. They were all contained in a file and she never went anywhere without that file. Now, she opened it and deftly fingered the sections until she came to the one she wanted. A quick glance at the list and she took hold of the one that resonated most clearly. So it was that she herself was almost as surprised as everyone else when she heard what she had to say.

'Poetry!'

Lord Coe raised an eyebrow quizzically.

'That is to say, a poet.' She was on her own now but this was an old party game in her household. You had to take an idea and run with it. You had to try to persuade everyone else that it was not only a good idea but the best possible idea in this the best possible of worlds. And doing this in the present boardroom was child's play compared to the Smith drawing room where by now everyone else playing the game could be counted on to be fairly blotto with wine and/or a spliff (but this was before her appointment to the Olympic Managing Committee. From that moment on spliffs and everything else that was remotely illegal were banned from the Smith household.)

Lord Coe's mouth twisted but it was hard to say how this related to his thoughts. Well, it was make or break.

'Yes,' she said. 'A poet. A poet laureate of sports. A poet who will write inspiring poems. Poems about victory. Poems about the challenge. Poems about pain. Poems about glory. Poems about …'

'A poet?' Lord Coe's voice showed clearly he was warming to the idea.

'Yes,' she said. 'A poet.'

'Of course!' Lord Coe was positively beaming. 'A poet. Poetry. Exactly. Quite. What a wonderful idea. Perfect.'

Now that an idea had somehow emerged and been accepted by the Chair, as they all referred to him, the other eyes regrouped and reconverged. Heads started to nod. Safer to nod than to shake. A shaken head had better come up with a damn good alternative idea. No-one wanted to engage in verbal fisticuffs with Mary Smith who had a reputation when it came to vicious in-fighting.

Lord Coe looked around the table with the smile of relief on his face. Poetry? Why hadn't he thought of that? Thank God for Mary Smith. But then he sensed that the idea had not quite reached its destination.

'But who?' he asked.

Before Mary could announce that she would draw up a shortlist of five leading poets and interview them personally, a soft Welsh voice broke into the proceedings.

'Oh I know a poet. Just the man for the job. If it's a poet you're looking for then Rowan Jones is your man.'

Ivor Jenkins was not often loquacious but when he had

something to say it was always to the point. He had earned respect and so it was that no-one thought to offer any other suggestions.

'Have I heard of him?' Lord Coe queried.

'Oh. You will. You will.' Ivor spoke with complete confidence. 'Rowan Jones is going places. Mark my words.'

'Well, if there are no other suggestions? Perhaps this ... what did you say his name was?'

'Rowan the poet. Rowan Jones.'

'Well, I suppose we'd better invite him up to London then.' Lord Coe said and passed on to other matters.

4.

In the kitchen, Bronwyn was bustling energetically about her chores. Bread was baking in the oven. A stew was gently gurgling on a hot plate. Chickens clucked around her feet. In the corner a pig lay snorting lazily, a cat curled on its back. Sunlight, a warm deep yellow sunlight, glazed the windows with the colour of honey before trickling in. Bronwyn opened the oven and with a dish cloth quickly rummaged in the interior checking that progress on the baking front was proceeding as it should. The yeasty smells of bread wafted round the room. When the phone rang Bronwyn plucked the receiver off the side counter and said: 'Yes? ... Yes!? ... Hmmm? ... I see no reason why not? ... Quite right too ... Yes he will! (this quite forcefully). He will not let you down. Thank you Uncle Ivor. I'll tell him right this minute.'

Then, when the conversation had ended, she replaced the receiver, a rather large and old fashioned receiver more in keeping with the period of her rustic cottage kitchen than with the times in which we live. In the short time it took us to note this fact, Bronwyn had written a note and put it in the beak of a rather stout duck. The duck waddled out of the back door and across the farmyard outside.

Out of curiosity, we follow. It becomes clear as we zoom up and away from the duck (in our mind's eye) that the farmhouse is set in a green and stunningly beautiful section of countryside not too far from cliffs and sandy coves and one of those warm, cuddly and cosy little fishing villages that does not exist outside a work of fiction. From this hawk's eye view, we watch the duck make its slow and bottom-waggling way across the yard and up a short lane to what appears to be — and indeed is — a very large greenhouse.

5.

Meanwhile ...
We can hear them a second before they come into sight, the thump thump thump of leather jackboots thudding down on flagstones and then thump thump thump on the concrete floors of a long echoey corridor. Louder. Coming closer. Thump thump thump go the boots in perfect unison. But there is another sound, a scraping, muffled human sound. Then suddenly we see them coming round a corner. First there is an officer. He is followed by a second officer. A woman. Her uniform is of a different cut. It is more form-fitting. And she has a form that is fitting. The creases of the shiny material glitter and sparkle from the light of the bare bulbs on the ceiling. She has the look of someone who has just

leapt bodily from an advertisement in one of the seedier magazines. In her hand is one end of a length of chain. The other is tied with a padlock round the wrapped and struggling form of a prisoner. Behind them there is a small platoon of soldiers.

'Halt!' The officer shouts and they all do a quickstep halt—again in perfect unison.

'Wait here!'

The officer then swivels round again and marches the last few steps to the door which he knocks on deferentially. The door swings open. He turns and beckons to the woman to follow with the prisoner. The three of them enter the room.

The room they entered was a vast space worthy of a president, and this was a room for not just any president but for the mighty President Osman Osmanakhian of Transcaucasia. Look on his mighty works and despair. It gave him great pleasure to sit behind his vast desk and watch whoever had come to visit him cross that vast area of unnecessary space. Space that existed simply to exalt him. Space that existed to emphasize his separateness from the world of everyday things. Space that allowed him to pace up and down theatrically when he needed to make a point. Space into which to hurl his unanswerable sarcasms. Space with which to amplify his presidential outrage. Almost always it was his anger. If he was not angry there must be something wrong with the world. If ever he should relax, smile, feel at ease with his fellow man, then that very day his kingdom would collapse. There would be uprisings and rebellions, rebellions and revolutions, revolutions and ... what was worse than a revolution? Volcanic eruptions. There would be revolutions and volcanic eruptions. Of this he was certain. So anger seethed and bubbled very close to the pyroclastic surface of the presidency, ready to spit and spew at any

11

moment. But the true secret to power was not permanent anger. No. It was changeability. It was unpredictability. It was the readiness to respond instantly in a way that no-one could have foretold. Keep everyone off balance was his motto.

Major Anatoly Pavlov set off across the vast expanse of carpeted space, followed by Captain Polina Polinka pulling and half dragging the poor, wretched, chained prisoner. President Osmanakhian jumped up from his chair as they approached his desk.

'Well?' he shouted.

'We have brought the prisoner.' Pavlov did his best to keep his voice from fluttering with nerves. 'He was found ...'

'She!' the word came out low and heavy with menace.

'Yes, Mr President. She was found trying to board a train. We arrested him ...'

'Her!'

'Yes, Mr President. We arrested her and brought him ... uh ... her back under guard.'

President Osmanakhian had heard enough. He waved his hand peremptorily and Major Pavlov swallowed the rest of his report. He waited to hear what was now required of him.

'Bring her here.'

Pavlov stood aside as Captain Polinka led the prisoner forward. Osmanakhian let his gaze slide approvingly across the slippery surface of Polinka's uniform before coming to rest on the bundle of humanity wrapped in sackcloth and chains. Osmanakhian waved Polinka away and stepped close to the prisoner.

'Oh Anna!' he breathed. 'Anna! Is this how you repay me?' He shook his head. 'After all I have done for you.'

Suddenly he whirled round and faced Pavlov with a towering fury.

'Release her now. This instant. This is intolerable. Is this how you treat our heroes? Our ambassadors? Our national representatives?'

He turned again to the prisoner.

'Oh Anna. How badly they have treated you. I will not let this happen again. I promise you.' He moved away to give Pavlov and Polinka room to unwind the chain and to release the prisoner from the sack that covered his ... er ... her head.

'But,' Osmanakhian continued, talking as much to the ceiling and the imagined television cameras, as to the prisoner. 'You must be loyal too. You must represent us at the Olympics. I can see it now. Gold medal. The first Olympic Gold medal ever won by an athlete from Transcaucasia. You will be famous. You will be a star!' Osmanakhian's hands had risen and were now pointing at the vaulted corners of the ceiling where light flowed in through stained glass windows. Slowly he allowed his arms to descend once again to his side.

The prisoner, now released, rubbed his ... er ... her wrists and flexed the various muscles of ... her body as she loosened up. Osmanakhian placed his two hands on her shoulders and looked deeply into the prisoner's haunting, haunted face.

'You will get new hormones, Anna, believe me, Professor Bogdanovich is working on it. You will be a new man!'

The prisoner gave a look of disbelief and gestured towards her groin.

'Don't worry. That will be rectified. The entire resources of the treasury will be at your disposal.' Osmanakhian paused and then whispered, 'If you bring us back the gold medal. If not ...?' The wave of his hand indicated that, in that case, there would be much impotent baying at full moons. Only now do we see, do we begin to understand something, of the tragedy before us. Anna is a woman with a man's body, or a man with a woman's ... well, what I'm trying to say is .... Once upon a time Anna was a man, a man called Dmitry, but now he ... er ... she is a woman called Anna. How else can I explain this?

But before we can completely resolve the issue the door at the far end of the room burst open and ...

6.

Despite the tropical undergrowth it hadn't rained here since, well, since forever. No question this was a season of drought. The words would not flow. The tap of thoughts was on trickle. Rowan sighed. There wasn't much good being a poet if he couldn't produce poetry. Maybe he needed to get out of the drowsy humidity and feel the native bleak, harsh and above all bracing coldness of his native land. Suddenly he heard a rat-a-tat-tat. Lunchtime already? It seemed a bit early. Though all this feeding of dried bread to the fish had left him feeling ... hmm ... you know ... just a bit .... He put down his pen and note pad, relaxed his furrowed brow and heaved himself to his feet. The dark green leaves slapped him as he strolled through the jungle to the door. He opened it and the duck waddled in.

The air outside was sharp and cool compared to the sweaty heat in the greenhouse so he quickly shut the door.

'What have we got here?' he asked and gave the duck a friendly stroke down its neck. 'A note?'

He read the note and his face gradually blossomed into an expression of stunned, whack-me-over-the-head-again amazement.

'Well, I'll be damned!' he said. And, lifting his eyes to the leaf-cluttered glass panels of the greenhouse roof, he closed them as wave upon wave of pure ecstasy peaked and crashed about him. 'Thank you Uncle Ivor. Thank you.' And then, thinking this was not quite adequate, he added, 'I won't let you down.'

At that moment the duck pecked him in the leg to remind him that she needed to be rewarded.

'Hang on Jemmy!'

The duck pecked him again and waddled after him as he hopped and limped to the pond where he extracted a soup scoop from underneath a plant. With this, he scooped up a bowl-size serving of pond sludge and dumped it in the tin can he kept handy for this purpose. Duck heaven.

Now that Jemmy's attention was elsewhere, Rowan re-read the note and shook his head in disbelief.

'Well I never!' he thought. 'Not ever, ever, ever.'

You could tell he was a poet. He had this uncanny facility with words.

7.

But as I was saying before I so rudely interrupted myself … Before we can completely resolve the issue, the door at the far end of the room burst open and two men—two identical men, two rather short, energetic, fluffy-haired, identical men in the white coats of research scientists, one of whom was carrying a replica Olympic torch and the other a bundle of papers—hurled themselves at the vastness of space in front of them, all the time shouting at each other.

'You tell him.'

'No, it's your turn.'

'I spoke last time.'

'No, you didn't. That didn't count.'

'Are you crazy?'

'And what have you got to tell me?' Osmanakhian's voice sliced through the bickering like a knife through the creamy goat cheese for which Transcaucasia is famous. 'Good news I hope.'

At this both men started nodding vigorously.

'You have solved the problem?'

Both men smiled broadly and started to dance up and down.

'Yes, yes, yes!' said the first (or was he the second?)

'The bomb ...' said the other. Suddenly they stopped talking and the room was for a second so silent that the ticking of a distant grandfather clock could be clearly heard. The two men looked round the room to see who might be listening. The first put his finger to his lips as a warning to the other but when he could see the other was going to speak again he slapped his hand round the other man's mouth.

'Grrmmphh!' said the other and mimed with his hands a large explosion. 'Boooom!'

The first scientist released him but made fearsome signs indicating that they had said enough. Looking at the President he indicated all the other people in the room and made it clear that what they had to say was secret. But the President's mind was on other things.

'Ah. The torch! And inside there will be a ...'

At this the scientists both put their fingers to their lips and the President too raised his finger to his beaming face. His voice was virtually inaudible it was so soft.

'A big explosion.'

Then throwing up his arms he shouted: 'Celebration!' The scientists too jumped up and down with excitement.

16

'We must celebrate,' shouted the president. 'How can we celebrate? Champagne? Ah no! We had a problem with the harvest. The new fertilizer ...' his voice wavered with indecision.

The prisoner leaned forward and whispered something in Osmanakhian's ear.

'Yes!' shouted the president. 'Excellent idea. This is an historic occasion and it must be commemorated for all time. Get the imperial photographer. Quick. Quick.'

The order echoed down a line of invisible guards till it reached the door guard who opened the door and bellowed the order out into the world beyond. Within seconds a photographer appeared and scuttled across the vastness of space loaded down with his equipment. Our attention having been diverted by this secondary activity, we find to our surprise that, when we now look at him, President Osmanakhian has changed his uniform and is now wearing the dress uniform of an admiral of the fleet.

'We need distinguished portraits of us all,' he called out. Which largely meant that he needed a distinguished portrait of himself. Then pictures of himself with Anna. Then pictures of himself with Anna and the scientists. Then ... On and on it went. Every possible arrangement of people. Major Pavlov to the left. Major Pavlov to the right. Captain Polinka to the president's right, to his left, on his lap. Only the very sharpest of observers would have noted the gradual disappearance of Anna from the group shots. Finally even Osmanakhian was sated.

'Enough!' He called out modestly, waving his hand in benign dismissal. 'No more! It's not as ...'

'The prisoner!' a female voice shrieked.

Captain Polinka was the first to note the fact that Anna was no longer among them. Heads turned left and right in

17

consternation. Major Pavlov looked first under the presidential desk then up at the ceiling. When he was sure the prisoner had not floated up on a bed of helium balloons he brought his eyes down again and found himself fixed in the headlights of the presidential stare. Suddenly, there was a noise from outside. Shouting. They all rushed to the window. They were just in time to see a mounted cavalry officer sprawling on the ground. Anna was astride his creamy white horse. She waved to the faces at the window before wheeling the horse round and galloping off across the vast square.

'Don't shoot!' shouted the president as the cavalry officer drew his service revolver and started to aim.

'Don't shoot!' he repeated. By now Anna had disappeared down one of the boulevards that fed into the square.

Turning to those around him President Osman Osmanakhian shook his head with a bleak sadness.

'Oh Anna!' he whimpered. 'Why do you treat me like this?'

Somehow, even in this short time, he had managed to change into the uniform of a field marshal, festooned with medals.

8.

It was evening. The gentle wash of waves lapped against the harbour walls of the small and unbearably cute fishing village. Lights and music both poured out of a friendly pub nearby. An almost tangible excitement pulsed through the air as Charlotte Church's scheduled arrival was imminent.

Rowan Jones was seated at the bar with a pint of dark beer in front of him. There was already a largish crowd and Rowan could be seen to be waving at a number of people. There was a podium and a band was tuning up. The background noise was already too loud for comfortable conversation. And then there was Charlotte herself—warmly Welsh, bubbly and buxom. She had to push her way through the crowd and Rowan found himself in close contact with the Church protuberances.

'Sorry,' she said as she forced her passage past him.

'No, no,' he said gallantly. 'My pleasure!' He beamed his delight into the following face—that of Miss Church's athletic ex-boyfriend and international rugby player, Gavin Henson, himself. Or someone who looked very like him. (Had they not separated? Somehow this snippet had slipped through the defences that kept Rowan Jones safe from the intrusions of popular culture.) Mr Henson, or whoever he was, was not pleased—at least he did not appear to be so. He gave Rowan a hard glare and Rowan suddenly felt an urgent need to turn back to the bar and savour his drink. When he saw the Henson-like person move on, he heaved an exaggerated sigh of relief. The barmaid had seen everything.

'Naughty, naughty!' she said wagging her finger at him. 'I'll tell Bronwyn on you.'

Rowan grimaced at the thought and in a loud voice tried to change the subject.

'You'll never guess what happened to me today.'

'What's that then?' she asked brightly as she poured a drink for another customer. The bar was packed today. Charlotte Church had brought them all out of the woodwork. There were people she had never seen before—like the funny crowd sitting next to Rowan who were pretending to be the Welsh basketball team. 'Did you ever see anything so ridiculous in your life?' she thought. So she only had half an ear to give to Rowan and missed what he said.

'What was that?' she asked cupping her ear.

'I said they've made me Poet Laureate,' he shouted.

'Poet what?'

'Laureate.'

'You mean Poet Laureate of England?'

'No, not that!' he shook his head and smiled. 'Just of the Olympic Games.'

'I didn't know the Olympic Games had a poet.'

'Me neither. Actually, I may be the first. Imagine that! The very first ever Poet Laureate of the Olympic Games. Me!' He laughed with becoming modesty at the absurdity of it but in his heart he was besotted with the pleasure of it. He'd been dying to tell someone. He was sure that she would now spread the news and soon everyone would know and he wouldn't have to explain it. People would point him out. 'That's the Poet Laureate of the Olympic Games,' they would say.

'I'm off to London tomorrow. It's going to be announced at a press conference. It'll be on the news, I expect. Imagine that. Rowan Jones the poet on the six o'clock news. That's something isn't it? My fifteen minutes of fame.'

To tell the truth, despite his feeble attempt to be blasé, he was still quivering with the excitement of it. He still hadn't got used to the idea. He was under no illusions. Uncle Ivor had swung it. Against what odds, against what competition he didn't know. Now it was up to him not to let the side down. It was up to him to make the most of it. This was his opportunity. A lifetime's make or break. If he fluffed this chance then it was back to ... he didn't know what. He'd never done anything else except poetry. Never been anything but a poet. He'd be one of those backwater poets that people sniggered at. He couldn't bear that. He wanted to be in the mainstream of cultural society, desperately wanted that more than anything else. Almost. Excepting anything to do with Bronwyn who was the love of his life. Thank God for Bronwyn. And as he thought these thoughts he had another sip of beer. He was so far into his thoughts that he didn't notice that the gorgeous Charlotte Church had begun to sing. Nor did he notice that the Welsh basketball team had heard what he had said and had gone into a huddle of discussion. In fact he only noticed them when they very nicely, very politely, but very firmly, displaced him from his bar stool and carried him to the back of the bar and out the back door.

'Hey up!' he said, taking it for a prank. He was still in celebratory mode. He had only just managed to grab hold of his glass and down its contents as they took him off. Someone took his empty glass from his hand.

'I'll have another ...'

Before he was able to finish the sentence he found himself being bundled into the back of a van. The door was shut on him.

'Hey!' he protested. 'A prank's a prank but really! This is ...'

The engine started and the van manoeuvred out of the pub car park. It was only then that he realized he was being kidnapped.

'Help!' he shouted but he knew it was pointless. There was no-one to hear him. 'Help,' he wondered. 'What are they going to do with me? I don't want to die.'

And then the awful realization came to him. He was going to miss his chance, his opportunity of a lifetime. If he was still a hostage tomorrow he would not be able to prepare a poem for the press conference.

'Ooooh!' he moaned in abject misery. This was really too awful for words.

9.

Lord Coe was beginning to feel edgy. He didn't like it at all. The press were even now seating themselves in the conference room. In a few minutes time he would be announcing to them, and to the whole world, that he had appointed an Olympic Poet Laureate, yet he knew nothing of this poet, what was his name? Ronald Jones? He instinctively looked at the table where all the speakers were to be seated. He caught sight of the name plates. Ah! Rowan Jones! Mustn't make that mistake. But where was the man? He should have been here long ago. He wandered over to Ivor Jenkins.

'Well, where is he?'

Ivor checked his watch against the clock at the far end of the room and shrugged.

'He'll be along soon. I told him. He's got all the details. You know how it is with poets.'

Well, no, he didn't know how it was with poets. At Loughborough, anyone admitting to have even read a poem would have been dunked in the Olympic-size university swimming pool. There were no such things as arty hearties. Not in his day. Not at Loughborough university. If you wanted to read poetry you went to Oxbridge. That's just the way it was. So when it came to poets or poetry or poems he was a lost soul. How had he got himself in this fix? That damn Mary Smith woman. Where was she? Ah there! He caught sight of her briefing Trevor whatsisname from *The Guardian* and thingamyjig Bradley from *The Times*. He mustn't let anyone see his rising panic as he felt a vital screw give. The edifice was shaking. Perhaps this poetry nonsense was a mistake. Perhaps they should just forget … But as he came close to Mary Smith he heard her saying confidently.

'And we've got a little surprise for you gentlemen—something to do with poetry. A touch of genius if I may say so. Ah Lord Coe.' She was suddenly aware of his presence just as he had been about to swerve away. 'I'll leave it to you to brief ...'

Ouch. Too late to back out now. He forced a smile.

'Ah yes. Poetry. Well, gentlemen, you'll have to wait until I let the cat out of the bag.'

'Shouldn't we be starting soon?' Mary Smith asked in a prompting things along tone of voice. Damn the woman, Lord Coe was beginning to shred beneath his urbane appearance. Damn the woman, damn the poet, damn the whole lot of them. He could feel it all slipping. Got to keep my nerve. Not long now. But he sensed he was beginning to skid. The ground beneath his feet was unsteady. It was as if he were dancing on banana skins, a whole crate of them. This job required more control, more controlled efficiency of movement than ever his running had. Control over his lips, his eyebrows—yes, the eyebrows in particular—and in fact all the facial muscles. He'd seen men afflicted with facial twitches. He sympathized with them. There was always that thought: there but for the grace of God go I. But there was also that sense of—what was the German word? Taking pleasure in others' discomfort. It would of course be the bloody Germans who had such a word. Schadenfreude. That was it.

'Hmm.' He murmured looking round the room vaguely. The press relations man was even now tapping the microphone.

'Ladies. Gentlemen. Testing. Testing. Perhaps we could all be seated ...?' The question mark hovered in the air as groups dissolved and everyone made their way to their appointed seats. His own in the middle of the head table, the press to their rows of folding seats facing him. Where was that damned poet? He'd have a few words for him when he showed up. It was going to put the Olympic committee in a bad light. If today they couldn't even get a single poet to arrive on time, he could imagine the comments in the press: could these people be trusted to launch the games on schedule? If the damn man wasn't here by the time they got to the announcement, there wouldn't be any damned announcement. That was that. He wasn't going to be made a fool of by a poet who couldn't be trusted to turn up at a press conference on time. The minutes were ticking by. There was a sound of muted expectation. Eyes were looking at him. It was time to get this thing rolling.

Just at that moment there was the sound from outside of tyres squealing and a distinct bang as something hit something else. Lord Coe decided to use up a few more seconds by going to the window to see what had happened. Below him was the forecourt to the building. He could see a painted Volkswagen van. Emerging from it was a tussle haired man so sloppily dressed he could only be the missing poet. Lord Coe glared down at him as Rowan patted the side of the van and waved to the occupants. There was no question in Lord Coe's mind. This was the poet. He watched the man rush up the stairs to the entrance. His heart sank. What had he let himself into? Why had he let himself be rushed into this early announcement? He sighed and made his way to the microphone where he was being invited to say a few words. He paused to survey the room, to show them he was in charge. He let his eyes roam in a relaxed way across the sea of expectant faces until the silence was such that a pin would have landed on the floor with a loud clatter.

'Ladies and gentlemen,' he began. 'In six weeks' time, the Olympic Games will once again ...' His voice carried with grave authority across the room, crisp and clear in every corner. He had a certain fondness for these moments of momentous gravity. He felt that they allowed him to show himself off with a certain heroic authority that went with his formal persona. To think, if he hadn't been so good at running, he would have been a nobody, he'd have been an accountant or a sports teacher, or whatever it was people did when they weren't being famous and organizing Olympic Games.

'So, it is our hope,' he continued, 'that we will have a joyful celebration of sport and athletics. That politics will be kept to a minimum and sporting passion will ...'

Suddenly the door at the far end of the room burst open and the short tussle haired, sloppily dressed man tumbled into the room, breathless and embarrassed.

'Ooops! Sorry!' he said. 'Didn't mean to interrupt. Is this the ...?'

'Ahah! There you are!' Ivor Jenkins shouted from the far end of the head table where he was sitting.

'Ivor!' the new arrival called back familiarly, with evident relief. 'Good man! So, I'm in the right place then.' He beamed at the fifty or so faces that had turned to inspect him.

'Come up here and take your place at the table.' Ivor indicated the empty seat beside him.

'What kept you?'

'Oh you know .... Big city. Traffic. Oranges and lemons. This and that.'

There was silence in the room as he walked round the back and down the side to the front. Lord Coe realized that he had lost the thread of what was admittedly pure and unadulterated waffle, and as everyone's eyes were glued to this strange and slightly misshapen man, he decided to introduce him.

'It seems now would be as good a time as any to

introduce our friend who has just arrived.'

Rowan Jones, seeing that all eyes were on him, put his hands together and bowed his apologies around the room.

Lord Coe gestured to the man at the end of the table.

'I will ask Ivor Jenkins to do the honours.'

Lord Coe sat down, feeling the pleasure of a man who has put another man on the spot.

'Serves him right,' he thought.

But Ivor was not at all discountenanced. He stood up and without the benefit of a microphone let his voice—a voice of great warmth and gravelly timbre—embrace and seduce his audience.

'It is my great pleasure to introduce Rowan Jones. Rowan, as you all know, is Wales's glorious up-and-coming poet; beloved of every man, woman and child in every valley and on every mountain top in the whole of our great country. I have known Rowan since he was born. I have watched him grow and mature until now he is like a fine and mellow wine. So ladies and gentlemen, here is our new and one and only Olympic Games Poet Laureate. We will be hearing great words from him throughout the Games. We will hear about the pain, the passion, the clamour and the glory. So let's hear a round of applause for Rowan Jones.'

The room erupted in clapping. Rowan stood up and bowed, holding his hands modestly in front of him. Then a voice could be heard from the heart of the room.

'Have you got a poem for us?'

Lord Coe smiled. He was half expecting Rowan to come up with an excuse. After all the man had only had less than a day's notice of the appointment.

'Yes,' he repeated the query to show it had official sanction. 'Have you got a poem for us?'

To Lord Coe's surprise the man plucked a sheaf of

papers from the inner pocket of his jacket.

'Well, I have something that I drafted on the way here, a little poem here for this august occasion. With apologies to our great national poet, the late Mr Dylan Thomas.' He cleared his throat and firmed up his back. He began to read.

Do not go gently into the swirling rain
As you pound the streets and feel the pain
The Olympic Games are here again
Four years after the last time in Beijing.

There was a muffled explosion of disbelief and laughter too sudden to be suppressed. Rowan could not think what had caused it. to calm his nerves he plunged on.

Round about and round about and round about you go.
The sand pits you jump and the javelins you throw.
And as your competitors run past you, you certainly know
Who's taking the very latest designer drugs.

There was a high pitched shriek from the far corner as a female journalist collapsed to the floor. Again he looked up from his sheaf of papers and wondered if he should stop. But all eyes were locked on him in a frozen spasm of unequivocal delight. I'd best keep going, he thought.

National prestige is the name of the game.
Which I, for one, think is a terrible shame.
Should it not be that he or she who gets the fame
Should not represent a country but only himself (or herself)?

By now the woman in the corner was wailing and hysterical. She needs a doctor, Rowan thought. Perhaps they're waiting for me to stop. He made an executive decision to ignore the next twenty three verses and just do the concluding verse.

So the Olympic Games should be open to all
No matter from wherever they come.
And if you ask me some questions about this
I certainly won't be dumb.

At this conclusion he bowed, waiting for that wave of applause that marks all great moments. But the room stayed silent as everyone waited for the storm to break. Lord Coe found himself open mouthed with astonishment. Had Ivor Jenkins not briefed the man? There was hardly a sensitive issue on which he had not uttered an heretical opinion. Drugs, nationalism versus individualism, accessibility. What an absolute disaster! He had to disassociate himself from this right now.

'You have set me up!' he shouted raising a threatening finger at Ivor Jenkins who was busy disclaiming all responsibility.

'No. No. This is not my doing. Who would have thought the boy ...?'

But by now the journalists were hurling questions at Rowan, who was looking slightly shell shocked at the furore. He certainly hadn't expected this.

'Are you saying that everyone should be able to compete?'

'Yes.' At least that's what he thought he believed. He wished his new friends could be there to brief and advise him. But they weren't. Be bold, he told himself.

'Yes. That is what I believe.' He asserted with all the strength at his disposal.

'Tibetans ...?' shouted another journalist.

'Yes, of course.' He answered. That was the best answer to any question concerning Tibetans.

'And what are you going to do about it?' asked another.

Do? He was beginning to get flustered. Poets didn't do things.

'I'm just a poet.' His voice had become unnaturally squeaky.

'So it's just fine words, is it? It's just hot air is it? You're not serious. It's just fancy words for a moment's notoriety. Is that it Mr Jones?'

'No, No. Not at all,' he protested. But that was the truth of it. But he couldn't leave it there. He could feel what was required of him and he wanted to meet that need. 'I will do everything in my power to help athletes from all nations who have been excluded from their national teams for any reason whatsoever.' And then he remembered something else his new friends had talked to him about. 'Or athletes who have excluded themselves. Why? Why should they exclude themselves? Well, because ... because they don't wish to represent the current regime of their country. And if we can't change the mind of the Olympic Committee ...'

Lord Coe could not believe what he was hearing. Who was this upstart? The room was in uproar as journalists surrounded the poet with microphones and cameras.

'Out! Out!' he roared. The door opened and three security guards came in. 'Throw that man out!' Lord Coe ordered.

Seeing the crowd they were being asked to deal with, they radioed for help and soon twenty or more security men were escorting Rowan Jones out of the building. The term 'escorting' should be given the widest possible stretch of definition.

'We need to look at the rules ...' he was saying as he was

heaved out of the front door and left sprawling on the steps amid a sea of camera flashes. He had a sudden, very brief, sense of identity with his carp and wished there was some murky pond bottom beneath him to which he could swim.

10.

The world's press leaped all over the story.

'The British Olympic Poet Laureate today called for a radical review of the power of national Olympic committees to choose their national Olympic teams,' said the New York Times front page story under the headline Poet Bursts Olympic Bubble.

'Rowan Jones, the Welsh poet,' announced an evening TV news anchor in Sydney, 'called today for a change in selection procedures for the Olympic Games. At a press conference organized by ...'

It was the same in Paris, Moscow, Tokyo and Brasilia.

'Poet attacks London Olympics,' said the Athens News with a certain unrestrained glee.

In every major news media in every major country this was front page news. All, that is, except one. For some reason the newspapers of a certain country lying south of Mongolia did not feel this was news worthy of attention. But that did not stop the news spreading quickly even there. A curious quiver of delicious outrage circled the globe—but no-one was sure at first who or what they should be outraged at. And then, as with most news, it disappeared from the media's memory banks. For the vast majority of the world's citizens this was a polyp in a deeply recessed part of the nostril. You could only reach it if you really needed to. It was more comfortable to just leave it be and get on with life. But there were some, a few, for which this news touched a very personal nerve.

11.

President Osmanakhian was striding up and down the vastness of his office wearing presidential jodhpurs and spurs that glinted and rattled with menace. In his hand was a riding crop that he slapped against his brown knee-high boots. On his head was the peaked cap of the dressage rider. Standing at attention beside a map of Transcaucasia stood a fearful, shaking Chief of Police.

'He cannot ...'

'She ...!'

'My apologies, Mr President. She, yes certainly 'she', cannot escape. All the border crossing points are sealed. Our men are waiting. There isn't a road, train track, airport or port that hasn't been notified. Hi ...' He dissembled a cough. 'Her photograph has been sent to all police stations. If she tries, she will be seen straight away and she will be caught. Of that there is no doubt. If she is hiding we will find her. If she is fleeing we will catch her.'

Osmanakhian stopped pacing and stood in front of the map deep in thought.

'And if she decides to cross along a mountain path in this remote region, what then?'

'Ah. Hmmm!' The Chief of Police made a number of thoughtful sounds. This possibility had not occurred to him but he dismissed it with a wave of his hand.

'Don't worry, Mr President. We will catch her. It is just a matter of time. We are completely on top of this.'

12.

'Impossible! She'll never escape!' The policeman who spoke was one of two sitting on a haystack on the back of an old jalopy that wheezed and coughed its battered way up a deeply rutted country lane. His companion laughed.

'That's what I told the captain too. She can never escape. We are on top of the situation completely.'

The truck bounced and sputtered but nevertheless kept on going. Looking back we can see how far the truck has come. Far below is the deep green of a well-watered valley, but up here we are beyond the tree line. The ridges are sparsely grassed. Ahead the land plunges down towards a swiftly-running river.

'We're here,' said the older of the two and rapped his knuckles on the driver's cabin. There was a flat area ahead, just room enough for the truck to turn. The driver brought the truck to a juddering halt. The mechanical effort of getting here had taken the vehicle to its very limits. Every rivet in its body seemed to have been shaken to within an inch of its life. The driver opened the cabin door and gingerly eased himself to the ground. Steam was billowing from the engine casing. The driver patted it congenially and put a cigarette to his mouth.

'Well?'

They each took out binoculars and, flopping to the ground, slowly surveyed the landscape. They shaded the glass lenses to ensure that there would be no glinting signal to anyone who might be on the lookout for them. They could see nothing at all. There was no sign that anyone else was occupying these heights. Down below, on the far side of the river, apart from what appeared to be an unoccupied sheep herder's hut, there was, similarly, no sign of anyone.

'So?'

They all nodded. The older one, who was wearing a corporal's stripes, appeared to be in charge. He rapped on the side panel of the truck. Two slow raps followed by three fast. This must have been the pre-arranged signal. Suddenly there was movement beneath the straw and a head appeared, then a body. It is the person we know as Anna.

13.

In his office, President Osmanakhian was now dressed in the uniform of a scout leader. His face was mottled purple with fury. The Chief of Police was shaking with terror.

'When ...!' he stabbed the Chief of Police's chest to punctuate the point. 'When we capture him ...'

'Her,' said the Chief of Police automatically and then realized what he had done. He closed his eyes to better envisage the consequences. Which form of medieval torture would the President choose for him?

'Her!' Osmanakhian growled and continued. The punishment was not waived, merely postponed. The rack? The wall of spikes? He would consider the details later. Now he had more urgent matters to deal with. 'When we have captured her, you will hang her upside down in the darkest dankest dungeon. You will cover her body with spiders and earwigs and worms and other nasty creatures. You will scrape fingernails down blackboards. You will let nasty children throw itching powder all over her. Do you understand?'

The Chief of Police shuddered at the thought. Not fingernails! Anything but that. But he was thinking of his own fate. He forced himself to open his eyes and face the President's fierce glare.

He nodded.

'I want her to suffer as she is making me suffer. Oh, how I want her to suffer.'

Osmanakhian paused, visibly at the limits of restraint — and yet restrain himself he did. 'But ... and this is very important. Not one hair on her head must be damaged. She must be punished but she must not be injured. She must run in the Olympics for the glory of Transcaucasia. Is that clear? I will hold you completely responsible.'

The Chief of Police nodded. 'Yes, Mr President. That is absolutely clear. She will be apprehended and I will have the darkest, dankest dungeon prepared for her immediately. Not a single hair on her head will be hurt.'

'Good! Now leave me. I have great matters of state to attend to. Tell the guard I must not be disturbed for the next hour.'

14.

Anna finally extricated herself from the straw and lowered herself with ruffled dignity to the ground. One of the border guards looked her up and down appraisingly.

'So, what do you think?' Anna asked sourly at this unsavoury inspection.

'It could have been a better job.'

'It was done by the very best surgeon in all Transcaucasia.'

At this the driver spat and pulled out a pack of cigarettes.

'And these too are the best in all Transcaucasia.' He offered one to Anna. She took it. The driver gave her a light and she inhaled. Her reaction was immediate. She threw the cigarette down on the ground and clutched her throat and chest.

'Exactly.' The driver smiled mockingly pulling another pack from another pocket. 'Which is why we only smoke these.' He lit two and handed one to Anna. She took it and sucked on it cautiously.

'So, mind if I ask you a question?'

Anna gave a flick of her head. She knew what was coming but they had put themselves out for her, let them ask away.

'Before this,' he waved his hand to include everything without including anything too particularly. 'Before this, you were a man who liked women?' It was a question. The situation had been infinitely more complicated but she didn't owe them the whole truth and nothing but the truth. All she owed them was a version of the truth that would do, that would satisfy their need to know—and best if that version of the truth aroused pity and a desire to help her. She nodded shortly.

'And he just ...?' The corporal mimed a snipping action at the level of the groin.

Anna nodded again curtly. The less said the better.

'And now?'

'What are you suggesting friend?' Her voice was deep but credibly feminine.

'Well, now that you're a woman?' he laughed as the implication was clear to them all.

'Do I now prefer men?'

The corporal nodded and smiled. That was what he wanted to know. And they had time to kill. Why should they not have some fun up here with no-one to see what they were doing?

'I hope you are not thinking what I am thinking,' Anna said.

The corporal laughed again and threw his cigarette to the ground.

'To hell with it,' he muttered. They waited till it was clear what he intended. But he intended nothing in particular.

'Come,' he gestured to Anna. 'I will show you the way to go.'

He took her to the edge of the ridge and pointed out the wooded hillside below.

'Stay within the trees. No-one will see you. When you reach the river, walk upstream for half a mile. You can't see it from here but there is a rope bridge. The smugglers all use it. If anyone stops you, just say Theo is your friend. That's me. No-one messes with Theo. On the other side, you need to make your way to ...' he mentioned the name of the town. 'There you will go to this address and give them this letter.' He handed her the envelope with the address. 'They will take care of you.'

Anna took the envelope and stuffed it into a pocket. It was time to go. She went up to the driver and shook his hand, patting his arm lightly to show her gratitude. She did the same with the other border guard, looking at him eye to eye so he should understand the depth of her indebtedness. Finally she turned to the corporal. She gripped his hand in both of hers. And then, to his wide-eyed astonishment, her lips were on his in a lip-crushing kiss that left him flustered and breathless. Without giving him time to recover his composure, Anna, laughing, let him go and picked up her sack. She threw it over her shoulder and set off down the path towards the wood and the river. The corporal ruefully wiped his mouth with the back of his arm. The driver and the other guard were looking at him with broad beaming smiles. He would never live this down.

15.

'Changeability!' He shouted into the emptiness of the vast room. He heard the sound of it reverberate for a few milliseconds before it was lost. 'Changeability!' He shouted again. There was no need to say more. This single word encompassed all wisdom — past, present and future.

And now he was alone. There was no-one to see him. If no-one could see him did he exist? He slammed his foot hard against a solid floorboard. The sound of it drifted off in a series of diminishing echoes until it too was entirely swallowed up in the silence. He was alone. How did it feel? Oh the luxurious and illicit pleasure of it! And oh the terror! The terrible, terrible fear of psychic oblivion. The pleasure! The fear! One. Then the other. Back and forth. Like an electric current. This was the battery of his soul. Oh yes!! Yes!! And now he must indulge himself. He pressed a bell. Immediately, from a secret panel in the wall, sprang a man with the most outlandish quiff of ginger hair. His lean and angular shanks sheathed in the tightest of tight grey suits. His shoes clacked across the floor as he made his way towards the presidential person.

'Danny La Zazu, as ever, at your service. Today we have ...' he snapped his fingers imperiously and immediately four short young ladies carried over a rather fetching pink outfit. In a trice, Osmanakhian was parading himself up and down the room, flouncing the long skirts this way and that. Someone handed him a parasol that was just divinely appropriate. He looked just like Audrey Hepburn in My Fair Lady.

'Don't I?' he asked the seamstresses for confirmation.

'Oh yes! The spitting image!' they shouted in chorus, well practiced over the years.

Another snap of the La Zazu fingers and four more seamstresses brought over an evening dress in gold lamé and in no time at all he was sashaying like Marilyn Monroe in *Gentlemen Prefer Blondes*. Oooh! He mouthed to invisible admirers and let his upper lip quiver just so.

'Changeability!' he said and winked, grinning with inordinate self-pleasure. He would have to think up a song. He felt the concept needed a Busby Berkeley-esque chorus.

'And this!' La Zazu once again snapped those imperious fingers and four more young, and very short, ladies brought yet another suit of clothes. This time it was an evening dress suit with top hat and a silk lined cape. The shoes click-clacked on the hard wood of the floor, just clamouring for a tap dance routine. He'd get the presidential choreographer on to it right away.

But time waits for no man and a shake of a lamb's tail later he was dressed in a dark grey three piece business suit. And then, as if sensing danger, noses quivered and suspicion turning to certainty, there was a headlong rush as Danny La

Zazu urgently ushered his gaggle of very short ladies into the gloom of the far end of the room where they disappeared back through the panel in the wall into the apartments that lay beyond from whence they had come. Not a moment too soon. The door opened and in came the First Lady, The Presidential Ornament. Oooh-la-la! The only person before whom he was entirely helpless. Followed by her diminutive, genetically shrunken, poodle. As she slowly and oh so elegantly traversed the vast space between the door and where he was standing she giggled and fussed with her hair while he stood still making deeply felt, deeply earnest, vividly expressive arm movements that said: 'My love. My one and only. My heart's desire. Passion of my life. My treasure. My sweetie-poo.'

Finally, she was there in front of him.

'You are having little, teensy weensy secrets from me, I'm thinking,' she tinkled.

'Nonsense, Tootsie.' The President got down on his knee to kiss her hand. 'Come here my lovely so that I can swoon once more in your presence.'

'Oh swoon! Swoon!' she muttered abstractedly, betraying the lack of conviction she felt.

'How sweet love is,' he said staring deep into the dark firmament of her eyes.

'I was thinking too we could go shopping. Just you and me. Hand in hand. Just like the old days.' She smiled at him that thin brave smile of the utterly bereft.

'Shopping?' Had she lost her marbles? Osmanakhian did not go to shops and department stores. When he wanted something—but was not entirely sure what that something might be—then shops and department stores came to him.

'You have no idea how bored I am,' she continued ...' I know it is a silly displacement activity and if I had a fulfilling and active sex life then I wouldn't give two figs for shopping—but as it is ….' There it was. Out in the open. It could not be avoided.

'This evening. I promise.'

'You're always promising, but you never …'

'This time I mean it. We will do everything.'

'Everything?'

'Yes. Everything.'

'Even?

'Yes, even that!'

'Oh darling! Darling!'

'Just one thing, my sweet.'

'Yes. Yes. What is it?'

'Just make sure my lederhosen are properly oiled.'

'Oh I will! I will!'

'And one more thing.'

'Yes?'

'The bagpipes.'

'Everything will be exactly as you like it.'

'I love you, my sweetie tweetie.'

'I love you too, booby-boo.'

And she blew him an air kiss as, very slowly, very elegantly and oh so very femininely, her hips swaying gently from side to side, she made her way back to the door.

16.

Rowan Jones, the up-and-coming, almost famous, modernist Welsh bard, was clutching his head in mental anguish.

'What have I done?'

Bronwyn Jones was stirring a pot of rabbit stew. At her feet and all around the kitchen there were animals of many species and hues. They were all inexplicably drawn to her. You could see the cats and the hens and the puppies and turkey and piglets and the lamb all made totally unnecessary excursions across the kitchen floor simply to rub themselves against her legs. A rainbow of subliminal colours radiated out from her, invisible to us but clearly visible to the animals. To us it is simply that she radiated that plump domestic contentedness that is so out of fashion—for the reason that it is unaffordable for the vast majority in our present stage of urban civilization. What will happen when even two incomes will be insufficient to raise a family? A conundrum for the future. For Bronwyn this was not an issue as she had no issue. Somehow it just hadn't happened. But she was young and no doubt babies would come along in their own good time. And when they did she would have the resources of the farm to depend on. She looked at her husband with pride and sympathy.

'You have done a good thing Rowan Jones. That is what you have done. You are a hero. Get used to that.'

'A hero?' Rowan groaned unable to convince himself this was true. 'A bloody fool is what I have made of myself.'

He started to lavish butter on a piece of freshly made toast that Bronwyn had put in front of him. 'And now what am I supposed to do?'

'You have your work, Rowan Jones.'

'And that is …?'

'You have focused the world's attention on abuses that neither they, nor you, if you're honest, were at all aware of. That's what you have done!'

'That's right. I did.'

'And now you can go back to what you were doing before with a clean conscience. You have done your bit.'

41

'That's right!' His eyes lit up for a moment. 'I can just go back to my lotus pond and get on with my poetry. Let the world get on with its own business.' But his mood having initially brightened now did a slow U-turn as he remembered the hours of staring at blank pages in his note pad while he rummaged around his head for ideas. The truth is he had rather run out of ideas. Or they'd gone into hiding. Or they were feeding on the boggy bottom of the murky pool that was his mind. Whatever they were doing, they were eluding him. When he'd had a cause he had felt the creative torrent bearing him along in its flood. Without a cause …? Bleak nothingness.

Just then there was a loud knock on the door. Rowan was not in the mood for seeing anyone and waved to Bronwyn to just ignore it but the knock was repeated and so Bronwyn wiped her hands on her apron and went to the door to open it.

'Are you at home?' It was a familiar voice but he couldn't quite place it.

'We are, of course,' Bronwyn replied hospitably and waved those outside to come in—and in they duly came. All ten of them. The Welsh national basketball team.

Rowan wasn't at all sure how he felt about them right now. On the one hand he was happy to help out in all things Welsh. On the other hand he had had his suddenly blossoming career almost instantly blighted—and it was all because of them. On the other hand (and three hands would have been quite useful at this point) he had got a great deal of notoriety which might, who knows, have an influence on things—though what things he didn't know right now, nor how they might be influenced, nor again how that influence might be beneficial. So it was with a cautious and mutedly expressed welcome that he stood up to shake their hands as they trooped in. And then, somehow, a voice started to intone a song. Another voice joined in descant style. Then a third. Soon there was a full throated rendition of Jericho.

Joshua fought the battle of Jericho … Jericho … Jericho.
Joshua fought the battle of Jericho
And the walls came tumbling down.
I know you've heard about Joshua
He was the son of Nun
He never stopped his work until
Until his work was done.

Rowan melted somewhat at this as, by now, the nine shortish, more obviously Welsh of the traditional sort, and the one tall darker man of less obviously Gaelic origins, (though nonetheless, Rowan was sure, just as Welsh as the others) had grouped themselves in an adoring circle around him.

'Well I just did my job,' he said modestly. 'That's it. Job done. Got the t-shirt and all that. There's nothing more I can do.'

At this the tempo of the song was ratcheted up a notch.

'You may talk about your men of Gideon.
You may brag about your king of Saul
But there was none like Joshua
At the battle of Jericho

At this the tall black player leant forward and pressed his finger into Rowan's chest and sang the next line unaccompanied.

And his mouth was a gospel horn

At this the entire choir repeated the line, all prodding

stern fingers in Rowan's general direction.

His mouth was a gospel horn.

Even Rowan got the significance of this.
'But I've done my bit. It's someone else's turn.'
In front of him ten men waggled their fingers in that universal sign of negation.
'But what else can I do?'
Oh Rowan Jones. The meek shall inherit the earth. We do not know the grand schemes that fate has in store for us. Even now, this very minute, your voice has gone round the world giving hope to the hopeless and something needful to the needy. Indeed, even now, less than a hundred miles away ....

Part Two

1.

The large house occupies a landscaped hill in front of and around which a large ornamental lawn sweeps away in a series of terraces on all sides. A small moat of gravelled driveway separates the house from the surrounding green. The large glass doors and windows of the house guard effectively the privacy of the interior, of which little can be seen from outside. It is a house in the Queen Anne style, which—as is the way with these things—has nothing at all to do with Queen Anne herself. If the shade of Queen Anne is able to look down and see this style, she will not recognize it, but I am sure she, the most invisible of the English monarchs, nevertheless welcomes the publicity.

It is a warm day. Cloudless. The sun beams down a muted glaze of well being. From the slant of the rays and the almost honeyed glow of the light we can tell that it is late afternoon. There are three men on one of the terraces seemingly suspended in an ocean of calm and silence. Only the buzz of insects, a buzz that noticeably increases as the sun continues its slow descent to the west, tells us we are not alone in the universe. Two of the men are dressed entirely in white while the third is wearing the dark coat and pin striped trousers of a butler.

As we approach the men in white, we see that they are fencers. It is clear that they have been at it for some time. They are wiping their sweaty faces with towels before once again putting on their protective masks. The one who is shorter, very much shorter, than the other draws our attention first. Naturally we feel sorry for a man who suffers such a disadvantage. We wait to see him lose—lose again, we assume—for the other man has the proud and somewhat arrogant stance of the athletically endowed. The fencers take up their positions and engage. What happens next bewilders and confuses us. We have to replay in our mind what we have just seen before we can credit it. It is the short man who has moved at twice the pace of his opponent. His weapon is spinning and vibrating and then suddenly, there it is—the point of his foil—firmly quivering in his opponent's breast bone—or where that bone would be if it had not been protected by a thick jacket.

Once the point had been acknowledged, Barnaby St John Smythe stepped back

'Sorry, old chap! I seem to have done it again.' He spoke apologetically.

'That's the sixth time in a row.'

'I must have caught you off guard.'

'No,' the taller man allowed himself a tight smile. 'No. The truth is I'm no match for you.'

'Nonsense. Just an off day,' Barnaby replied.

The two men took off their masks and, having also taken off their gloves, gravely shook hands.

'A little refresher, what do you say?' Barnaby signalled to the butler. Perkins had already prepared the drinks. He moved forward with a tray. The two fencers mutely toasted each other and then quickly emptied their respective glasses. Perkins obligingly provided a refill.

'It's becoming more and more difficult to get a decent match these days.' Barnaby shook his head.

'I'm sorry I wasn't able to put up a better show.'

'Good God man,' Barnaby expostulated. 'You're the best fighter I've tangled with in the last twelve months. I wouldn't say this to you otherwise. But the fact is, I'm running out of competition. How can I improve if I haven't got anyone to fight? I'll have to give it up and take up knitting or something of that sort.'

'Well, the Olympics are coming up. Why haven't I seen your name in the selection competitions? That's where you should be—fighting with the very best, not against has-beens like myself.'

'Come. Come. You're doing yourself an injustice. But as for the Olympics, well, it's no good. I tried it once. Too much toadying. Too many silly rules. Health and safety nonsense. What is this obsession with risk aversion that we are lumbering ourselves with? And this height business is a bit annoying. They keep overlooking me. No, I'm just not a team person. It's not my cup of tea at all.'

Perkins poured a third glass of champagne. There was a slight pause as they considered the ever deepening yellow of the sunlight which heightened the colour notes of everything they could see around them. It was in fact an utterly magical moment as a late spring afternoon eased itself into early evening somewhere in the very heart of England.

'Well,' said the tall man at last and then paused to cough and clear his throat before continuing—a device he had learned so long ago he had forgotten it was a learned technique for capturing the attention of his audience. 'There's a Welsh chappie who seems to be organising something different—a sort of fringe Olympics where anyone can join in—the more the merrier.' He smiled deprecatingly. 'You might want to contact him.'

'Now, that's what I call a jolly good idea! Make a note of that. What's the fellow's name?'

'Rowan Jones,' Perkins murmured. 'The well known Welsh poet. Author of the much appreciated poem: Wherever Thou Goest, There Too Go I, which he wrote, if I'm not mistaken, as a homage to the Millennium stadium in Cardiff.'

Barnaby looked at him with a show of mock outrage.

'You're just showing off, now. And besides, what is this false modesty? You know that you are never mistaken.'

'I try to be of service.' Perkins bobbed his head and unobtrusively faded back a few steps, not desiring to impose too much on the conversation of the two fencers which now strayed to other subjects—African bees, Indonesian orchids, the latest outrageous statement ululating from the inner sanctums of Ten Downing Street and so on and so forth.

2.

Anna had reached the river with little difficulty. It had in fact been a delightful stroll downhill through the woods. The dry ground underfoot was such a pleasure after the hard cement of the ... he shuddered at the memory of his recent experiences. And that bloody man Osman. How had he ... she ... allowed herself to go along with this mad scheme. Drink! That was it. Osman had got him—and at that time he was a him—drunk. No doubt there

48

were drugs involved. His ... damn it ... her psychic defences had been stripped away. And now? Was it really reversible? She hoped so. These were some of her thoughts as she found herself alone and free. By the time she reached the river she was jauntily and lustily singing to herself.

The river itself was not fordable at this point. It was a tumbling, foaming mountain torrent. She now had to strike uphill for a mile or so till she came to the bridge. When she got to it she found it was being used. A smuggler was going home with his unladen pack animals. Anna gave him a wave and followed him across.

'Going far?' asked the smuggler as she came abreast of him.

But Anna just smiled and waved vaguely ahead. She then put muscle into her legs and sped ahead quickly leaving him far behind.

3.

Meanwhile, somewhere in Siberia ...

The large metal prison gates swung open and a man was half carried, half dragged by two guards. The man was shivering uncontrollably. His clothes were little more than filthy rags, and although he had a hat with ear muffs it was a thin and barely adequate affair. The guards, themselves were warmly wrapped in enormous greatcoats and had hats with thick glossy fur. They slung him to the side of the road and hurled a solitary piece of baggage after him. He watched dully as they headed back into the camp. The gates closed behind them. Slowly he picked himself up and taking up his baggage he walked unsteadily down the road towards the railway station, visible about a mile away across the bleak landscape. When the train eventually came the man managed to squeeze himself into an already overcrowded carriage. Now it was just a matter of time. Either he would reach his destination or he would die. It mattered not at all to him which of these two fates was destined to play out. He crawled under a bench and made himself as comfortable as he could. Over the next hour he was crippled by a pain that ripped through every muscle and joint. This pain was an old friend. This was the pain of thawing out.

Some days later he was still alive. This surprised even himself, who had thought he was beyond surprise. He had quit that first train for another. Then quit that too and hopped on the back of a truck. Then he remembered there was a lift in a van driven by a rather fat man. He couldn't stop staring at him. A fat man! How wonderful! Fat! How long had it been since he had seen fat, beautiful, white, wobbly fat. The driver had noticed his interest.

'Something wrong. Comrade?'

'No! It's just that …' But the effort was too great. Some things just could not be explained.

'Beautiful!'

'What's beautiful?'

'You.'

'Fucking poofter!' The driver slammed on his brakes and the van juddered to a halt.

'Get out!'

He had got out. No point in trying to explain. Must not make that mistake again, he told himself.

Eventually, he found himself where he wanted to be. It was just a walk now—ten miles of flat grassland. If he was lucky someone would come along and give him a lift. If not …? And of course, maybe they would all be gone, the people he knew. Five years was a long time. People grow old. People move on. People die. But he had no choice in the matter. He had nowhere else to go. He started to walk. He was lucky. A farmer on an ancient and somewhat rickety motorised cart gave him a lift and after half an hour of bone shaking, dropped him off at the cabin. Standing there with his bag in the dirt he looked around him. He could see there was someone working with horses in a pen beyond the cabin. This was the moment of truth. He walked slowly towards him. He saw the man turn and look at him. He just trudged on. The man was looking hard at him now. And then it seemed there was a shock of recognition. The man physically jerked backwards, then started to walk towards him, moving faster.

'Ivan Rimsky-Radetski?' Hesitantly. 'Ivan? Is that you?'

'Ivan Rimsky-Radetski?' thought the man in wonder. How long had it been since he'd been called that?

'Boris Nikoalyevich?' he managed to croak. 'Is that you?'

The men came together by the side of the cabin.

'Ivan!'

'Boris!'

Then they embraced. Ivan had forgotten what it felt like to be hugged by a friend. But he knew he was home now. He was among friends.

'Come!' Boris tried to move Ivan towards the cabin. 'You must be hungry. Thirsty. When did you last drink decent vodka?' But Ivan's gaze had settled on the horses.

'Ah yes! The horses,' Boris murmured and tried again to deflect his friend.

'Come. The horses can wait. Tomorrow is another day.'

Ivan snorted. 'If the Gulag teaches any wisdom it is this: there is only now, today, this minute. Yesterday is gone.

Tomorrow may never come.' He was already walking towards the pen. 'But maybe I have forgotten the feel of a horse between my legs.'

Boris shook his head and followed. Six horses wheeled away from them. Ivan watched as the horses milled about, unsettled by this new energy, this new man.

'Untrained,' Boris murmured unnecessarily. Ivan saw everything. His eyes sucked in every detail from the muscle in the belly and the lightness of the step to the colour of their sweat matted coats. It had been so long since he had smelled this tangy odour of horse. It filled his own lungs and belly with a hard desire. This was the heady perfume of his soul. He dropped the bag that he had been carrying and climbed, without thinking, to the top of the stockade fence.

Boris knew when he was defeated. 'All right then,' he said. 'Maybe it will take a horse to beat some sense into your thick skull. Take one. Any one. See if you still have it in you, but take care now,' Boris warned.' You are not as strong as you were.'

Ivan ignored him, keeping his eyes fixed on one, then another, of the horses, seeking out the horse he would choose. This power to choose, to impose his wishes, was intoxicating stuff. When had he last been able to raise his eyes and meet the world on his own terms? Yes, his very own terms. He felt the rush of power coursing through him, a release of pure energy from his loins. What did he care if the horse bucked and twisted? It was no matter if he was thrown. He'd been thrown many times. But no horse had yet beaten him. Not Ivan Rimsky-Radetski.

Then he made his choice. Satan. The name was an obvious one for the jet-black colt with the blaze of white across his face. He waited his moment aiming slyly first for another of the horses before finding the grip of his fist fasten on the hair of his chosen one's mane. He swung himself up and with a flick of his head to Boris forced the horse towards the gate. Boris opened the gate just enough for Ivan to force his own mount out of the corral and then hurriedly shut it again to prevent the others from following. By the time he had lashed the gate shut again Ivan was a cloud of dust in the distance. Boris took out a cigarette and lit it.

'Well, well, well,' he thought with a smile in his heart. 'Ivan Rimsky-Radetski!' The best horseman he had ever known. He never thought he would see him again. Not after that stunt! He laughed as he recalled what he knew of it. Making a fool of the President's number three mistress. It was bound to get him into trouble. Why on earth had he done it? Of course she'd been a proud bitch and had deserved every inch of the humiliation he had extracted. But still! The man had too much pride. One day his pride would kill him. And now that he thought of it, hadn't the woman recently been accused of some crime or other? Was it drugs? Of course she said they'd been planted. And maybe they had been. What had been her real crime? Treachery? Some branch at least of the ultimate crime, worse even than the crime of disloyalty, the crime of being an obstacle in the way to something else that was desired. So, was that how it was? Her friends were now enemies; her enemies were now friends. Ivan had been thrown in prison. Now he was thrown out of prison. And so the world spirals from one absurdity to another.

Boris spat into the dirt. He was well out of it. Here with his horses there was little to disturb him. Horses come. Horses go. He pocketed the difference. It wasn't much of a living but he was happy. Who else could say that? He looked up and saw Ivan racing his horse back across the flat field towards him. Then they slowed to a trot and a walk. Ivan was grinning. He had lost a few teeth, Boris noted, but the fire in the man's eyes were the same. At the sight of the pen, the black horse skittered sideways a few steps but Ivan was having none of it. He had a firm grip on the mane and a stick that he had acquired in the other, with which he gave the horse a flick. There was no question who was boss. Ivan rode him to the gate and Boris once again opened it just sufficiently to let them in.

'Now, about that vodka.' They both grinned. This was a day for getting royally drunk. Boris picked up the flea-bitten bag and putting his arm around Ivan's shoulder led him towards his simple cabin.

'You have not lost your touch.' It was the simple truth and he intended it as such. 'Do you plan to contact the Olympic Committee? They have not found anyone who can replace you. You could walk straight into the team. I am sure they would welcome you with open arms.'

Ivan looked at him sourly wondering what streak of evil had entered his friend's spine, weakening it till it bent this way and that with the prevailing political wind. But the twinkle in Boris's eye reassured him. No. This was a test. A final temptation. The offer of reconciliation. And of course Boris was probably right. Perhaps he could walk back into the team. Give him two days with a horse, any horse, and he would make it do what he, Ivan Rimsky-Radetski, wanted him to do. This was not a problem. A horse would be found for him. If that was what he wanted. But he had no desire to forgive. He would not be gracing the pastures of the Russian Olympic Committee anytime soon. If he did he was not a Rimsky-Radetski.

'Drink!' Boris said and handed him a tumbler of the smokiest vodka he had seen in a long time. Ivan sniffed it suspiciously but the sharp smell of its authenticity tingled his nostril. He placed a shotful on his tongue and cradled the fire.

Then he let it slowly trickle down his throat as he savoured it. Ah yes! This was the real thing.

Boris poured out another glassful and then, remembering something urgent, wagged his finger excitedly in Ivan's face. He got up and went to a shelf where there were some papers. He sorted through the pile until he found the newspaper cutting he wanted. He thrust it in Ivan's face.

'Read this.'

It was a two-paragraph story—pointedly gleeful at the embarrassment caused in Britain by Rowan Jones's antics.

'This Welsh poet,' the journalist crowed, 'says that he will do everything he can for any athlete who wants to represent himself rather than his country.'

Ivan let the thought settle in him. This was his technique. He did not leap to judgment. Neither agreement nor disagreement. The thought simply lay there in the cool waters of his mind. After a while it would become clear how he felt about it. It didn't take long. The rightness of the idea was clear. Slowly a smile, hard and sardonic, cracked open his lips.

'Yes. This is good. I will go to him.'

With that decided they sat down to the hard and serious business of getting drunk.

4.

Rowan Jones had been doing some reading. In fact, as he wondered the fields, he carried the book with him until he found a willing listener. She was familiar with Rowan and was not unduly startled when he sat down in the grass next to her.

'Did you know that the Olympic Games are officially dated from 776 BC but that they probably were held for several centuries before that?'

She was used to Rowan sitting down and saying whatever he wanted to say on whatever subject. She had learnt to just look at him approvingly and let him talk. He was, after all, completely harmless.

'And from then on they were held every four years at Olympia in Greece until they were finally abolished in 393 AD by the Roman Emperor, Theodosius I who considered them to be unchristian. Isn't that interesting? Probably because the athletes ran naked. Christians didn't like that for some reason. What God had made was not considered to be good. Hmm! Chew that one over! But I digress.'

His listener stared at him gravely for a moment, her large eyes glistening with a benign and accepting intelligence. Rowan melted under her gaze. Then she lowered her head and turned away to look at the view of the green, wooded and undulating countryside spreading away from them.

'The modern Olympic Games,' Rowan spoke hurriedly now as he didn't want to lose his audience, 'were only re-established in 1896 by a Frenchman, the Baron de Coubertin, and they were held in Athens in 1896. It was Baron de Coubertin who founded the International Olympic Committee. Since then the Olympics have been held every four years.' He paused to check she was listening before continuing: 'Well almost every four. Not during the first and second world wars, of course.' Rowan paused again. 'Well, actually, I say 'of course' as it if was of course. But the ancient Olympic Games were held every four years whether there was a war or not. In fact wars were stopped for the games, rather than stopping the games for the wars. Now, that's what I call civilized!' Rowan's agitated look as he hurled these words into the wind was too much for his listener. She heaved herself cumbrously to her feet and moved away, her large udder swaying heavily from side to side.

5.

The time for the President's press conference came and went with no sign of President Kenneth M'Gunzu himself. He was known to hold the press in complete contempt so this was no surprise. M'Gunzu held everyone in complete contempt, or so it appeared. How else explain his equanimity in the face of economic collapse, his extravagance in the face of unbearable poverty and his refusal to see what everyone else could see: that his country was being ruined. Violence was endemic, indeed it was orchestrated. Famine was rife. People were starving to death. And yet the old man continued to play the little games designed to bolster his prestige and sense of self-importance.

The press, meanwhile had been ushered to a roped off area of lawn and left there without chairs to sit on, or shade to keep off the midday sun. There were maybe thirty men and a handful of women, most of whom were representing the local media. A press conference in the midday sun? What message was he relaying? Only mad dogs and Englishmen? Nor were there any drinks to slake their thirst. Thirty minutes went by, then another ten. Still no sign of M'Gunzu. The first to crack was Sam Gorman, stringer for the Herald Tribune and a number of other major American papers.

'The hell with this!' he muttered to Eric Weatherall, who handled most of the British press. He lifted his leg over the cordon but was prevented from lifting the other by an armed guard who started to push him back into the enclosure. Sam resisted and there was a temporary standoff.

'You tell your president,' Sam muttered fiercely into the soldier's implacable face, 'that if he wants to tell America anything, he can do it himself. I'm getting the next plane out of this godforsaken hole.'

He turned to his colleagues.

'Gentlemen, and ladies, you have my deepest sympathy. Adios.' He waved goodbye and again turned towards the soldier. This time he smiled and gestured that he only wished to take his leave. But again the soldier pushed him back with his gun.

'What?' Sam Gorman protested. 'Now, you've got yourself a story buddy. Journalists forcibly detained by lunatic president. What's your number?'

He pulled his pen and note pad out but before he could note down the soldier's number he was gun butted in the stomach.

'Jesus!' he muttered from the kneeling position he found himself in. But before he could say anything else, there was a rustle of movement at the front entrance to the large white colonial era building that was still known officially as Government House. The Old Man, as M'Gunzu was familiarly called, had appeared at last. He had across his shoulders the skin of a lion. It had been draped elegantly over his light tan suit. He walked slowly and heavily in a way that justified his thick black, gold topped walking stick. A small podium had been set up at the edge of the lawn in front of which were four microphones. The president was helped on to the podium by one of the three stunningly beautiful female assistants who accompanied him everywhere. An official busied himself making sure the microphones were at the right height while the president looked across the lawn to the gathering of journalists. He gave a signal and the soldiers guarding the journalists now made it clear that they were expected to approach the President at a jog. Weatherall gave Gorman a hand to help him get to his feet and together they strolled after the others.

'Ladies and gentlemen of the press,' The President started. 'I denounce corruption. I denounce inter-tribal warfare. I denounce poverty and violence ....'

But you have heard all this many times before, and this was long ago.

⁊

At the very moment the President started to speak, two truck-loads of troops sped into a village some two hundred miles away. It was a peaceful village going about its placid daily rhythms. In the heat of the day there was little activity. Men sat in the shade of trees discussing cattle and goats and water and the movements of the tribes around them and the crazy old man M'Gunzu and all the other things that men talk about. The women, meanwhile, were gossiping in their gardens and the shaded entrances to their homes. They talked of their children and cooking and who was growing up and who was ready to be married and the complex inadequacies of their men and all the other things that women talk about. And then the two truckloads of soldiers arrived.

It was clear straight away that this was not a friendly visit. The speed of the trucks alone showed aggressive intent. But at first it seemed just to be a lack of friendliness. The soldiers did not belong to the N'gongo people, as they did, so could not be expected to be friendly. But when two trucks drove from one end of the village to the other, and then, when one of them turned round and came back until it was back again at the entrance, it was clear that something was up. The men rose to their feet to observe the progression of events more clearly. But they were not yet alarmed. The woman clutched their children and ran with them to their huts. And so it stayed for fully ten minutes: the two trucks idling at the two ends of the village.

Kono was eleven years old, not yet old enough to be with the men, but old enough to be impatient of the younger children. His mother was suckling his youngest sister. He was the eldest of four. The other two were playing a game with stones in the corner of the hut.

'What is happening, Kono?'

'I don't know. The soldiers have parked at both ends of the village.'

Perhaps Kono's mother had an inkling of what was about to happen.

'Kono,' she said. 'Run secretly to the forest. Don't let the soldiers see you.'

'Why?'

'Don't ask. Just do what I say. Now!'

Without a second glance, Kono slipped out of the hut and ran as fast as he could, staying bent low, until he reached the forest. From there he saw everything unfold. He saw the two trucks suddenly race towards each other but this time they were shooting indiscriminately at everything that moved. The men were hopelessly exposed. Not one reached safety. In two minutes it was all over. Then it was the turn of the women. The huts were torched and the women and children came out screaming only to be cut down.

When the troops eventually departed, having looted what little there was to loot, Kono came out of hiding and slowly checked each shack to see who had survived. Of all the two hundred or so people in the village that day, only Kono was still alive.

The shock of it was too great. He felt his spirit retreat into himself, as deep as it could go. What was he to do? Where was he to go? He remembered once one of the elders had waved his hand to the south saying: 'The world goes on forever.'

Kono gathered up what few things he thought might be helpful—a little food, something to carry water in, a spear—and, when the heat of the sun had dropped, he set off, heading south.

That was many years ago. Kono walked. Kono stole food. Kono did odd jobs. Kono grew. Kono listened and learned. Kono learned to spit and smoke and drink and shout bad words and to fight (fight to the death if he had to). And above all Kono jogged along on his long skinny legs, loping and running. And he learnt to do all the bad things people do when there are no other pleasures. And the years passed. And Kono grew. And Kono learnt the ways of the world. And so it was that one day he found himself in a shebeen with a desire for a drink and to listen to some music and to hold a girl in his arms and to obliterate the pains of that day. And he had money in his pocket to pay for these pleasures. And he was happy to take what pleasures came his way. He knew how to enjoy them thoroughly. Because you never know when two trucks of soldiers might suddenly turn up. You didn't want to die with too much money in your pocket.

Business was slow in the shebeen and the shebeen mama was leaning on the bar swatting flies. Kono sat on a bar stool and puffed smoke rings. The only other man in the bar was the kind of well dressed hit-on-you man that Kono liked to stay well clear of. But this one wasn't trying to sell him anything. Or at least he didn't think so. Not yet. He was reading a newspaper.

'Ho!' he suddenly called out. 'Listen to this. Some guy here says, he's writing about the Olympic Games, says 'no glorification for nations', it's only individuals that count. Well, what do you say to that?'

Kono wanted to just ignore the man and go back to his drinking but the thought stuck to him with great force. It seemed to him it was the most important idea he had ever heard.

'That man say the truth!' he said. 'The truth!'

'That so?' The suited man gave him a slow inspection. 'I say he is crazy!'

Kono jumped to his feet and began to pace the length of the bar.

'He is not crazy man,' he said at last. 'He is wise. I understand him. Hear me! I tell you this! I will run for me. I will run for my people, I will even run for you.' He pointed to the man and then at the shebeen mama. 'But I will not run for my country. I have no country. Country means nothing to me.'

The shebeen mama lifted her head off the counter.

'You will run for me?'

'Yes. I will run for you.' He pointed at the man. 'And I will run for him. For this bar. For this township ...'

'Hold on,' the shebeen mama shouted. 'Forget about all them. Just me and my bar. Will you run for me?'

'Sure.'

'Can you run?' the man in the suit had hauled himself to his feet and was giving him a close inspection.

'Yes, I can run. I can run all day. I may not be fast but I can run and keep on running.'

'I guess that makes you a marathon man.'

'What's that marry thing?'

'Marathon. Twenty six miles or thereabouts. Can you run that far?'

'I'm just warming up.'

'Wooah! I think we need to trial you. If you can run

twenty six miles in a couple of hours then maybe we got something.'

The shebeen mama looked him hard in the face. She had never been a beauty and she was now well into her fifties but he was mesmerized by the intensity of her expression.

'If you can do it. I can pay for it.'

Kono's ears pricked up. There was money in this running thing? Hell, maybe he needed to take it seriously.

'Tomorrow. You plot the route, I'll run it. You time it. Let's see.'

And that's what they did. It was thirteen miles to the next town so they agreed he should run there and back. The shebeen mama would do the timing and the man in the shiny suit, whose name turned out to be Wilfred, ('Always have to have a European name if you want the white people to give you work. And if they don't give you work, they don't give you money.') would follow in a cab driven by a friend — just to make sure there was no cheating.

And so that's what they did. And when he was back two hours and twenty three minutes later, they reckoned they might have themselves a runner.

'How fast do the top runners go?' the shebeen mama asked.

'Two hours something small, like two hours five minutes, something like that.' Wilfred was eyeing up Kono with something close to admiration. 'But that's at the end of a lot of training — our man hasn't had any training and he just goes and runs a very respectable time on a pot-holey road in shoes no self-respecting runner would touch.'

'What do you mean 'our man'?' The shebeen mama growled.

'Hey, he's my man too! I was there when we discovered him.'

Kono just smiled. He quite liked the idea that he belonged to someone.

'And now we got to get in touch with this Wales man,' he concluded.

'What Wales man?' The shebeen mama's voice was heavy with suspicion.

'You see! That's why you need me. Because you are ignorant of the world. But me, I read the papers. I know things about the world. And one of the things I know is this here Wales man that is organizing an Olympic Games for individuals.'

'You didn't say anything about no Wales man ....'

Well, we'll leave them there. The conversation went on long into the night but one thing was clear. Kono would be needing a passport.

6.

We must not forget Anna. She ... er he ... no, we were right first time ... has found herself in a small town. She studies the paper that she was given. There are no street signs. What need is there for street signs when everyone knows where all the streets are. Only strangers don't know the names, and who wants strangers poking their noses round the place? Anna is forced to ask someone for directions. The woman takes one look at the address and waves for Anna to follow her. They go down a narrow alley until they reach a thick wooden door. The woman bangs on the door. When it is opened, Anna shows the letter and she is welcomed in. So that's Anna dealt with. For now.

7.

Meanwhile, in a small clearing in the forests that hug the southern Appalachians, on the Tennessee side of the Blue Mountains ridge, a sweating and very uncomfortable police deputy was mopping his brow with the white napkin that he otherwise held raised in the air to establish as clearly as he could that his intentions were entirely peaceable.

'Cousin Jeremiah?' he called out again. The sound of his voice was swallowed up by the trees. A squirrel skittered across the clearing. 'Squirrel's on steroids' he smirked, thinking how he would retail it later at Doreen's. He studied the tree line carefully. In these forests there were bears and deer and bobcats and muskrats and woodchuck and opossum, and red and gray foxes. And of course, the state emblem itself, the fucking raccoon. And skunks as well no doubt. There was even European wild boar that had been set loose here back before anyone knew any better—and when was that, he snorted to himself. And out there too was his cousin Jeremiah with whom he had shared many a bottle of whiskey and more than a few pipes of the illegal weed. Those were the days when they were young and wild and didn't know no better, before the ways of the world had impacted on them, forcing them along their separate paths.

Everyone hereabouts was a brother or a cousin. Cousin Randy was sheriff. Cousin Chandler was mayor. Cousin Doreen ran the local tavern. But cousins didn't always see eye to eye. And cousin Jeremiah least of all. Truth was, Jeremiah was just plain ornery. And dangerous to boot. No-one was handier with a bow and arrow than ole Jeremiah. Why he didn't pack guns, no-one knew. Except of course he told 'em it made them lazy. With a bow and arrow, Jeremiah used to tell them (this was way back when he deigned to talk to folks), you are on even terms with nature. Any fool can blast away with a gun but it takes a clever fool to fell a deer with a bow and arrow. And it takes the special kind of fool that Jeremiah was to face down one of them big beefy wild boar. There was something in the soil of Tennessee they liked and they growed big. Jeremiah had, from an early age, delighted in heading off into the hills to go head to head with the boar.

'Smartest animal in all God's creation,' he'd say as he got a few of his 'amigos' (that was the word he always used) to heave the carcass off the back of his pick up. 'Next to man, of course. And he's smarter than some of them that I know.' He'd laugh at that. How he'd got the carcass on to the truck in the first place, no-one ever found out. If anyone asked, Jeremiah would look at him in an amused sort of way and say 'pulleys' like it explained everything. Everyone felt he was laughing at them so no-one asked anything more. And that surly, sly smile on his face didn't do him any favours. And then the damn fool started to fool around with Pastor John's youngest wife. Jeremiah's view had been that one wife should be enough for any man. But Pastor John was of a renegade Mormon sect and had a different way of seeing things. And since Cousin Randy took a benevolent view of differing marital arrangements, nothing was done to rectify the situation. 'Hell, Joe,' he would say when pressed on the matter. 'We got Muslims and Jews and Hindus and Cherokee and Apache and Mormons and every kind of Christian fundamentalist known to man. Best I don't stir my stick in that passel of maggots.' Course, when Jeremiah took it into that head of his to whip Pastor John to within an inch of his life (he had taken exception to Pastor John exercising his rights over said wife—as it was his rightful duty to do even if she had required 47 stitches afterwards and would never again be quite such a pretty sight) then the sheriff had to get involved.

❧

Joe Adams called out one last time. It was hot up here—or maybe it just seemed hot. He sensed he was being watched but hard as he stared at the surrounding bush, he could make out nothing human. Jeremiah's cabin was just across the glade beyond the small stream that cut its way through the grey rock of the hills. Just as he reached the edge of the water an arrow smacked into the earth near his boots. Joe stopped. He was relieved to see a man step from the trees about fifty yards away.

'Howdy Cousin,' Joe said.

'I told you never to come up here no more.'

'You did, Jeremiah. You did,' he said placatingly. 'Just that Cousin Randy done told me to tell you he's expecting you to turn up at the courthouse on Tuesday next. Nine a.m. sharp. He wanted me to tell you in person. Otherwise he will be forced to take you in.'

Jeremiah spat.

'You go tell Cousin Randy he can kiss my ass.'

Joe laughed.

'I already told him that's what you'd say.'

'So, you got any more business up here?'

'Guess not.'

Joe had done his job and he had no desire to try the famously thin patience of Cousin Jeremiah Trout. But he could not resist making one last dig.

'But you're losing your touch. If that was aimed at me I reckon you missed by a mile.'

'Who says I missed?' Jeremiah had waded across the stream in three strides and pulled the arrow out of the dirt. He waved the dead rattler in Joe's face.

'Hey!' Joe was surprised.

'Two more steps and you'd have stood on it. That would have been the end of Cousin Joe.'

'Well, I'll be darned. That was one hell of a shot. And I never knowed there was a snake there at all.' He wiped his brow with the napkin before pulling his hat on firmly. 'You're good enough to be in the Olympic Games I reckon. You never thought of trying out?'

'I don't go in for that big business shit.' Jeremiah said as he skinned the snake using his Bowie knife. 'I'm the best. That's just a fact. I know that. Why do I need to go out and show all them foreign dudes how good I am? You know the problem with this country? Even the goddamn Republicans are pinko pansies.'

'You wouldn't be interested in this then?' Officer Adams had taken a newspaper cutting out of his pocket. This had been his real mission. The sheriff had read the story and had said to him:

'You take this up to that ignorant jackass, our cousin Jeremiah Trout. See if you can't lure him out of them thar woods.' He made to put the cutting back in his pocket.

'What's that then?'

Joe Adams handed the cutting over and Jeremiah started to read, forming the words slowly: 'With athletes and sportsmen and sportswomen participatin' as individuals.' He nodded his head and looked up at Adams, 'I'd go along with that. What's that man's name? Rowan Jones? Maybe I'll just drop him a line.' Again there was a pause as he digested the information. Finally, with something akin to embarrassment, he spoke again.

'Now, Cousin Joe, maybe you can help me. I don't rightly remember. Which state is Wales in now?'

8.

Rowan had found another listener.
'Baron de Coubertin,' he paused to check if he was being followed. There was a slight nod of the head so he continued. 'You know, the man who founded the modern Olympics. He was asked to express his philosophy and this is what he said: 'The most important thing in the Olympic Games is not to win but to take part, just as the most important thing in life is not the triumph but the struggle. The essential thing is not to have conquered but to have fought well.' Isn't that, well, the way it should be?'

His listener, knowing that the response was perhaps not what Rowan was looking for, looked sadly back, then twitching his pinkish ears, snuffled and went to roll in an alluring pile of horse manure nearby.

'To strive, not to have strife?' he murmured as though he may have hit upon an important idea.

9.

Meanwhile, in a town somewhere in North Africa, night settled on the narrow alleys as one by one the lights of the town were extinguished. But the light of the moon hanging over the town like a pregnant lemon was bright enough to cast cold shadows across the pebble stones. Beyond, in the blackness of space, the stars were like grains of glittering sand. It was after midnight when the doorway set into a massive wooden gate creaked open. A head peaked out, looking left and right to check that all was clear. Then the figure of a woman emerged with a bicycle. She mounted it, clicking her shoes into the pedals, and was off, up the slight incline of the cobbled alley.

For Ayesha this was a moment of heady liberation. She was revealing herself for who she really was in this public space. She felt naked, exposed, cleansed. Once she had left the cobbles of the town behind she was on smooth asphalt. It was two hundred miles across a high desert plateau to the next town but she was not going that far. She had only two hours of freedom—the freedom to exhaust herself, to feel her muscles expand and contract as she pumped her legs up and down. It was the watch on her wrist not the speedometer on the handlebar that dictated her training.

The bicycle itself was beautifully light and balanced and each part was the very best money could buy. She went through the gears making sure the derailleur was working as it should. When she was satisfied all was well, and when she felt her muscles were warm and supple, she began to harness her back and belly as she forced the pace—pushing herself harder and harder. There was no-one else out here. And when occasionally she saw the lights of an approaching car in the distance she would stop and flatten herself behind a boulder till they were gone. This was how it had been this last year.

But unknown to Ayesha this night was different. Her activities were not the secret she thought they were. After she had left the house, five figures detached themselves from the shadows and made their way to the gate.

'We will wait here for her return,' said the leader

'If her family refuses to maintain its honour, the whole town will be dishonoured,' whispered one of the others, as if needing once again to justify the deadly deed they were resolved on.

'Sssh!' The leader waved his hand urgently to silence him and then indicated where they were to lie in wait, then sat himself down by the doorway.

But, unknown to them, they had been observed.

Ayesha's father, Abdul, sat in his room talking to God. It was an old conversation.

'And what did you think would happen when you bought her the bicycle?' Allah asked with a laugh. Abdul shrugged and shook his head.

'She is a headstrong girl. What is the harm of it? I thought. No-one need know.'

'And how could they not find out? Would she not ride it?'

'Only at night I said to her, when no-one can see.'

'And before that you gave her an education, as if she were a son.'

'Did you not agree with me that this was right and good?'

'I did.'

'Was not Khadijah, the first wife of the Prophet, blessed be his name, an educated woman?'

'She was,' Allah acknowledged.

'They came to see me today.' Abdul recalled the delegation of neighbours and leading members of the community who had come to his carpet shop that afternoon.

'And?' Allah asked out of politeness for all is known.

'They told me it was outrageous. That I should put her away.'

'Put her away?'

'Or *they* would.'

'And how did they justify this?'

'It was a matter of honour, they said.'

'Not a matter of evil?'

'Evil?' Abdul sighed and shrugged.

'If honour can only be maintained by evil, what kind of honour is that?'

'They say it is what Allah demands. They said 'She insults us all with this behaviour. We are here to punish her.' Those were the exact words.'

'So!' Allah laughed. 'I am so weak that I cannot carry out my own punishments? I need idiots like them to maintain morality?'

'The Imam was with them. He too supports them.'

'That old grey beard!' Allah laughed. 'Am I so stupid that I will only speak to mean, bitter, old men?'

Abdul went over to the window and looked out on the street. He had half a dozen security cameras covering the key points of entry and he could see on the glimmering monitor in the corner of his room the five men awaiting Ayesha's return.

'If the imam is not to be trusted, who can I trust?' he asked again, as he had asked before and there was no change in Allah's answer.

'Trust your own heart.'

'But what about the rules?'

'But nothing!' Allah's retort was sharp. 'Is that all there is to life, to follow a set of rules? Listen to me and listen very carefully. If each generation is less wise than the last, then you have already fallen far from the true source and your wisdom is not to be trusted. On the other hand, if each generation has the potential to be wiser than the last, why should old men not learn from their children, from their very own sons and daughters?'

This was further than Allah had gone before. Was he to listen to Ayesha and do what she required? He felt the heavy weight of what was being asked of him. He felt it like a stone in his soul. He had given Ayesha an independent and enquiring mind. No. Not true. Allah had given her this mind. He, Abdul, had merely helped her nurture it. He had done this freely and with love for this precocious daughter of his who had shown her intelligence from an early age. If this was a fault it was his fault. If there was glory in it then he would be honoured. But it was not an easy thing this thing that was being demanded of him. To let Ayesha be free to choose her own journey in life, this was the difficult thing. And now her choices had led to this displeasure. She had to go. This was clear. She had to get away from this town. It was fortunate that he had the resources and contacts because she would have to go now, this very day. But where was she to go? Her brother Ibrahim would know. But time was speeding by and Ayesha's life was even now under threat.

అ

Up on the plateau, Ayesha checked her watch. She had come as far as she could. It was time to turn round. If she had known that this was to be her last night in the desert perhaps she would have let her eyes rest for a moment on the heavens but the moon was even now sinking towards the horizon. She had already pushed on a quarter of an hour too long. Now she would have to make this her fastest descent yet. She felt the large gear wheel resist for a moment the pressure of her leg. And then she was moving, and each circuit of the pedals was easier than the last. Soon she was racing down the long straight road as if riding for her life.

అ

Abdul woke Ibrahim.

'Father, is something the matter?'

Briefly he explained the situation and handed him a

hunting rifle.

'We must deal with them now, before Ayesha returns.'

So they made their way quietly to Abdul's study where Ibrahim saw the situation on the monitor.

'Let me take care of this, father.'

'We will both take care of it.'

They approached the door in the gate as quietly as they could. The click of the key in the padlock was unavoidable so as soon as he heard the click, Ibrahim snapped the bolt back and pushed the door open. Then he stepped out into the street followed by his father. Pointing their guns in both directions they covered the five men.

'Rascals! Scoundrels!' Abdul shouted in a loud and menacing voice. 'What are you doing here?'

The leader of the men slowly got to his feet and drew a dagger from his belt. Seeing this the others followed suit.

'We are here to protect our honour,' he sneered.

'You will drop your knives.'

'Curses on you!' One of the men spat.

'No, my friend,' Ibrahim laughed. 'The curse is upon you. It is the curse of stupidity and ignorance. It is a lifetime penalty. Now, I will not repeat myself. Your knives or I will shoot you, Allah be my witness.'

Their knives clattered to the ground.

'Have you not got homes to go to?'

'She insults us all with this behaviour. We are here to punish her.' It was one of the followers who spoke, not the leader.

'Away with you,' Abdul growled. 'If you insult me any further, I will punish you.'

'Be careful, old man,' the leader laughed. 'You have a shop. A shop needs customers.' He spat. Then waving to the others they picked up their knives and walked off, swaggering.

This last riposte met its mark. This was a fight that Abdul could never win, not if he wished to do business.

Just then Ayesha sped round the corner and braked to a skidding halt.

'Father!' she was surprised to see him in the street. 'Brother! What's happening?'

The tensions of the last few hours suddenly broke through.

'Ayesha!' Abdul exclaimed. 'Ayesha! You must stop this madness! You are bringing scandal to the family.'

'Father! I don't understand. How can it be scandalous to ride a bicycle? Is Allah so mean? He gives us legs and then tells us not to use them?'

'But why, Ayesha? Why? Everyone is talking about it? Everyone is laughing at me behind my back? There is a man, they say, who cannot control his scandalous daughter. My business is suffering.'

'Why? Because I want to challenge myself. I want to be strong and healthy so that I can be a good mother for my future children.'

'Children? You talk of children? But who will marry you?'

But Ayesha remained obstinate. The clear whites of her eyes were like glistening pearls as she looked him straight in the face.

'I want to race in the Olympics.'

Her father shook her head. They turned and walked back into the house.

'How can you be an athlete when the people don't want to see a woman athlete? The Olympic Committee is under the control of the religious authorities now. They are the voice of the people and for them women should stay at home to cook and care for the children. Isn't that what Allah intended?'

'Is that what I intended?' Allah asked with a smile but only Abdul could hear him.

'Father!' Ayesha fell to her knees and clutched at his robe. 'You know I love and honour you. You let me grow and blossom by giving me freedom. You educated me. You let me inform my heart and my mind so that I could make distinction between what is good and what is not. Now I must express to you what is in the heart that Allah gave me. It is my deepest desire that I will compete in the Olympics. I must do it. I do it to bring honour to Allah, to my nation, to my town, to you.' By now tears were coursing down her cheeks. 'I will find a way to do it.' She turned to her Ibrahim.

'And you, brother, are you the same? You think I should stop? In the name of Allah?'

'Is Allah so mean? Is Allah so small? I do not think so. I think Allah is great. I think the works of Allah are great. And man is great. And women are equal to men in the eyes of Allah. This I believe. And Allah glories in the achievement of good things.'

'In any case she must go.' On this Abdul's mind was made up.

'Where am I to go?'

Ibrahim took from his robe a piece of paper and handed it to his father, who read it without comment and then, nodding thoughtfully to himself, he handed it on to Ayesha. As she read it her eyes grew bright with excitement. When she had finished she looked from her father to her brother and back again. 'This place Wales …' she asked, her voice shaking with sudden hope. 'You will help me to get there?'

10.

Anna has managed to attach herself to a goat herder. When the goats leave town for the upper pastures Anna follows. The first part of her journey to the west will take her up into the bleak plateaus of the country. This is not the quickest way to traverse the country but it will be the safest, for her.

11.

Meanwhile, at a running track on the outskirts of Bückeburg, a small town in central Germany, there is a provincial level track and field competition. The 200 metres sprint is just about to start. The runners are bent low, having put their feet into their starting blocks. The race official barks out a noise and they all rise, straining at the point of release until they hear the 'pop' of the gun and they're off. It's only then that we see the blond runner in the third lane has artificial legs. Or rather he has curious flat carbon fibre extensions to his knees that look not unlike miniature skis. The runners have rounded the bend and are headed up the straight. It is a close race but the blond man has overtaken the early leader on the inside lane and by the time they cross the finish line he is a yard in front. He coasts to a halt, his arms raised and grinning with pleasure. Then he waits for the time keeper to report the winning time. Is it good enough? The other runners slap him on the back as they pass him. And then the time is called out. It's inside the Olympic qualifying time.

Fantastic! That's just what he needed. He walked over to his trainer who was just finishing a telephone call on his mobile.

'Yes. Yes.' He spoke into the phone. 'I'll tell him. He's right here. OK. I'll get back to you.'

He ended the call and looked at the keen, expectant face in front of him.

'Karl, good race.'

'It was inside the qualifying time.'

'Yes. I saw that.'

'So?'

'So, not good news. The answer's no. They say the legs give you an unacceptable advantage, that it's not fair to normal athletes.'

'Aren't I normal?'

'You know what I mean.'

'What do I have to do to convince them? We've shown them the experts' calculations. They say I get no benefit at all. They have measured the length of my stride. They have measured my heart beat. They have measured my muscle contractions. They have measured everything. The conclusion is clear. No advantage.'

'I know. But I'm not on the committee.'

'Now what do I do?' Karl muttered despondently. 'After all this training, what do I do?'

12.

Rowan had cornered another listener.

'Do you know what Article Six of the Olympic Charter says? No? It says this: The Olympic Games are competitions between athletes in individual or team events and not between countries. I repeat, between individual athletes and not between countries. That's what it says. That's exactly what it says.'

After half a minute of considering this information the lamb went off bleating in search of its mother.

13.

The large hall was full of gymnasts. Men hung in mid air, the muscles of their arms bulging hard as they fought to control the two metal rings they were each gripping. There were six of them fighting to see who could hold out longest. Below them, lithe girls were swinging their way through their routines on the uneven bars and the mat: twirling handstands, rolls, spins, somersaults, cartwheels and all the rest of it. Men whirled themselves up and over and around the pommel horse. All in all it was a dizzying display of activity. The only sounds were the shouts of trainers and the smack and whack of human body parts slapping against plastic foam mats.

Jade Lee had just completed a tumbling act when the coach tapped her on the shoulder and pointed to the far door.

'Director Chung wants to see you.'

Obediently, Jade went to put on her track suit jacket and trousers, then headed for the door. She wondered what Director Chung wanted to say to her. In her mind it could only be one thing. A yes or a no. Was she going to be in the team or not? By all rights she should be. She had earned her place. She might not be number one. Her good friend Phoenix Lim was certainly number one. She was the one the whole country expected to get the gold medal. No, she was not number one. Nor perhaps was she number two. Maybe not even number three. But somewhere in there between three and five. That's where she belonged. And they were taking a team of six girls so there should be no question that she was going. So what did Director Chung want to talk to her about? Maybe he just wanted to congratulate her in person. So she walked quickly and lightly across the open yard to the administration block where Director Chung had his office.

'Ah there you are, Jade.' He said when he saw her. 'Come in. Come in.' He smiled benevolently. 'You have been training hard I see.'

She nodded. She was always tongue-tied in his presence. She was very much in awe of his authority.

'It would be a pity if all this training came to nothing, do you not agree?'

Jade registered that this was not a promising way to start a conversation. She didn't know whether to nod or shake her head. Instead she did neither, waiting simply for the situation to clarify. 'I am finalizing the team and I have only one space left. The question is should I take you, Jade, or should I take Miss Pang? What do you think?'

What was he talking about? Lily Pang was a sweet girl but she just wasn't in Jade's class.

'I don't understand.' Jade's mind was in turmoil. 'I've always placed higher than her in the national games.'

'That's right. That's why I would prefer to take you.'

'I don't understand the problem.' Jade was beginning to panic. All this work over so many years. The gradual ripening of her skills, her strength, her style. All of this was now hanging in the balance. But in the balance against what? Some pretty girl called Lily Pang who had never placed higher than eighth place in the national competitions?

'You must reward me.'

'Reward you?' So this was about money? She didn't know whether to be annoyed or relieved. 'You know my family is poor. We have no savings. How much …?'

'It's not money, Jade.' He smiled and shook his head at the thought. 'I know you are poor. I know how important it is for you to go to the Olympics and to do well. Your whole life depends on it. Your career. Your future. It is impossible to say how important it is for you. All I ask is a small favour, a trifle.'

'What?' she could barely croak out the word. A dark nameless premonition hovered over her. Director Chung approached her now with his hands out. He cupped her face and she could feel the cool dampness of his palms. He bent his face down towards hers and for a second she was inclined to turn her face towards his and open her mouth and let him do to her what men did to women. He was right. Her whole career lay in the balance. The well-being of her family was at stake. She had dedicated this body to years of training for the pleasure of representing her country. Why should she not let her body be used in this other way too, if that was what was required? But while her conscious voice was saying these things to her, justifying her acquiescence, darker undercurrents of feeling were rising in her gorge and it was all she could do to avoid vomiting in his face. Her face twisted in disgust and she spat at him. Did she really spit in his face, she wondered afterwards as she raced out of the office, out of the building, grabbing her bag and clearing out her locker because she knew that was the end of her career, the end of her hopes.

She had to tell her mother. She had to beg her father and mother for their forgiveness. Why couldn't she have just let him touch her where he wanted to touch her? Why couldn't she have touched him where he wanted her to touch him? These were simple acts. But even as she berated herself, she also knew that she had had no choice, no volition in the matter.

And her mother understood everything.

'They will cancel your passport.'

'I know.'

'So you must go now, today.'

'Where?'

Her mother shrugged.

'Anywhere.'

Then she remembered something. She picked up the newspaper. There was a sneering article about a silly poet in Wales.

'Go to him,' she jabbed at the article. 'He has a good heart. He will help you.'

She thrust her life savings into her daughter's hand.

'And take this. But you must go now. There is no time.'

And they hugged each other tightly, knowing that it would be many years before they would see each other again, if they ever did.

14.

Anna has long since left the goats behind. She is now traversing an infinitely bleaker zone. She trudges through deep snow surrounded by grim, icy mountain tops. Ahead of her is a glacier with all its treacherous crevices. But there is no way back. On and on she must trudge. It will be touch and go if she makes it to the other side.

15.

The waters inside the lagoon and outside could not be more different. Inside, the colour is a light crystalline azure. Beyond the reef the water is the darkest of blues—so dark it seems black. Inside, the waters are still and flat. Outside, there is a swell, a constant heaving, swaying. There is continual movement. This lagoon—known as Maniara to the local people, the place of shells—is one of the largest circular reefs in the entire Pacific. A vast volcanic basin. But it will not always be like this. The waters are rising. The one island that had been habitable, no longer is. The entire community has been forced to relocate to the neighbouring island which is more mountainous, just visible on the horizon. But not quite everyone has left. One man still manages to eke out a living here, still maintains a cabin on the shrinking acreage of the solitary island that still manages to sprout trees. This lagoon once thought of itself as a nation, with its own culture, its own language. Now it is little more than a memory, a dreamscape of nostalgia, a place that soon will be no more, that is destined to become a legend, a myth, a dream.

But the shells in the lagoon still attract visits. A sailing canoe was even now heading towards the gap in the reef. The three man crew consisted of two grizzled, hard-faced sailors who had weathered many an island passage in these seemingly so flimsy boats. The third was a young lad, about eighteen years old. He was the only one who was not heavily tattooed. Finding the gap in the reef was a tricky process but the old men remembered it well and this was the day they were handing that knowledge on. So it is. So it always has been.

Knowledge passes on from one generation to another.

'Is he still here?' asked the boy. He could see nothing. Then one of the older men pointed. It was blinding to look into the distance with the dazzle of the sun off the surface of the sea, but the boy forced himself to stare in the direction the finger was pointing. And then he saw it, a movement. He kept his eyes on it a long time, never letting it go.

One of the older crew grinned a gappy grin, his few remaining teeth like black stubs in his gums.

'Well, screw a dung coloured octopus.' He laughed at the absurd sight.

'Who is it?' the boy asked.

'It's him!'

'He goes by the name of Brother-of-the-ocean-turtle,' said the other man.

'Yeah,' old gap tooth grinned. 'But we call him Mad Mike.'

The boy turned back to see the man they were talking about come speeding towards them. It was the strangest boat he'd ever seen—a long, skinny contraption—and the man was sitting with his back to the front of the boat. How the hell did he know where he was going? And he was pulling on two oars, one on each side. One hand one oar. Not like a canoe.

'What do you call that thing?' he shouted as Mad Mike shipped his oars and glided across the smooth unruffled surface towards them.

'It's a single scull mate.' There was pride in his voice.

'It's fast.' The boy reached out his hand tentatively to touch the gleaming polished wood.

'Yeah. As fast as a barracuda on speed.'

Old gap tooth grinned.

'Y'ever think of racing it?'

'Against who?' his grin mocked them. 'You?'

'Nah,' the old man laughed. 'Not me, mate. But, you know, some kind of competition.'

'You think anyone's gonna come here to race against me?'

'Reckon not!'

They all laughed at the craziness of that idea.

'Nah! You'd have to go to them, I reckon.'

'Well, I was thinking of representing my country at the Olympics,' he grinned. It was a grim grin that squeezed out all the humour in the words. 'But my country went and sunk on me!'

They laughed again at that. Then, when they had stopped laughing, Mike leaned over and spat into the sea, then slowly and deliberately cleared his nostrils one at a time.

'Yeah,' he said at last with a sigh, 'I wouldn't have minded going to the Olympics and that.'

Again there was a silence as they contemplated the death of desire.

'Funny thing,' said old gap tooth. 'I think I heard something recently about the Olympics, now what was it? Oh yeah! Some fellow on an island called Wales ...'

16.

Rowan was crouching outside a hole in a grassy embankment.

'It is an important part of the mission of the Olympic Committee to encourage and support the promotion of women in sport.' He was reading aloud from a pamphlet 'This is in order to help the implementation of equality between men and women.'

A rabbit poked its nose out of the hole and deciding that Rowan was harmless came all the way out.

'Don't you find that interesting?'

The rabbit looked at him for a moment and then hopped off.

17.

Meanwhile, in Paris … Paris, France … Marguerite Moreau was sitting in her usual chair in the small café that she frequented. In one hand was a cigarette and in the other a small glass of cognac. The law on smoking had changed but she had not and the bar keeper didn't give a damn as long as he didn't lose his license. Across the table from her was a famous philosopher whose name I can never recall. But take it from me he's famous. You'd know him if you saw him. He had long flowing locks with an elegant wave. It was the sort of hair you have to wash every day, especially if you're famous, as he is, and could be photographed any time, any day.

'The Americans are crazy!' she said. Actually, she said something like 'Les goddamn Yanquis sont fou, absolument fou.' But since everyone for a hundred or so miles in every direction agrees with this sentiment she gets little mileage from it. The philosopher made a face. His fame trapped him. He could not allow himself to utter anything banal (what is the French for banal?) or he would be laughed at and even he could see that any comment on the goddamn Yanquis was going to come out banal, no matter how true or to the point. A certain sense of ennui pervaded the scene. I don't know what the French for ennui is either but it was threatening to become terminal. But all that was about to end. Suddenly President Nicolas Sarkozy appeared at the doorway followed by several dozen flunkies. He stormed in. He kissed her on both cheeks before she could defend herself. A man placed a small podium on the floor so that he could stand on it and so appear taller, which he did.

'Marguerite, Cherie,' he appealed to her with both arms spread out, a scene illuminated by the rapid spatter of camera flashes. 'We need you. Your country needs you. I need you.'

Marguerite stood up in a dignified manner and gestured dismissively, in a typically Gallic way, as she spoke.

'My country is a whore. And you, sir, have a wife!'

But Sarkozy was at his oleaginous best.

'Nationalism is vulgar, I admit, Marguerite, but think of the honour. You are our best pole vaulter. The best in the world. You are a miraculous runner, an all round athlete. The heptathlon is yours. You are bound to win four golds, maybe five. This has never been done before. Not in athletics. Not by a citizen of France. Not by a French woman. You just have to participate. Go to London and show those damn Rosbifs what we can do. What is the point of all the training you have done if you are not going to go to the Olympics and win? Just do it! Do it for your own fame! For glory! For history! For your grandchildren! And yes, for La Patrie.' From somewhere in the background came the sound of the Marseillaise and they all remained at attention until it ended. Even then, when silence had returned, no-one moved. The entire weight of attention was placed on Marguerite's shoulders so that she could feel the terribleness of this weight, this weight of national expectation. But Marguerite was a proud woman. When she spoke the words emerged coated in that sexy, smoky huskiness that bespeaks a profound depth of cynicism, an immense weariness with the way things are.

'If there is a point, Nicolas, may I call you Nicolas? If there is a point to all my training it is this: it is to be the best, to be recognized as absolutely the best, and then not to participate. Can you understand that?'

Sarkozy recognized defeat. He threw his hands up in the air, then shrugged expressively for the cameras and walked off, taking his entourage with him, one of whom deftly picked up the mini podium and took it away with him. Marguerite remained standing looking sad that she had won, almost forlorn.

'And yet I would give anything to be there.' She murmured. Only her companion heard her. But he was sympathetic. He understood the complexities, if not the paradoxes of the human heart.

'Perhaps you have not read this,' he said and passed a newspaper to her, pointing to a particular article. Marguerite read it with an intense expression on her face.

'So,' she said finally. 'That would be très amusant, n'est-ce pas?'

18.

Anna has made it across the glacier field and has now reached the edge of a vast escarpment. Below her the land plunges towards the empty weathered rocks below. She unpacks her bag and rearranges the contents. Then strapping the bag to her back again she gives a brief prayer to a God who is not there, she supposes (for if He was there how could He stand by to let what happened to her happen) but to whom she nevertheless she feels it incumbent to recognize at these moments of critical action. Then she takes a twenty yard run, hurls herself off the cliff edge and hurtles down. One … Two … Three … she counts. Then pulls the cord. At first, for a heart stopping moment, it appears that nothing is going to happen. But then the chute comes streaming out and her descent is suddenly made less rapid. The wind catches it and she sails out from the cliff side, circling round. There a new thermal catches the chute and on she flies. Fifteen minutes later she lands five thousand feet lower than she had been. Here she finds herself on the edge of a wide and barren landscape. For us, contemplating it at a distance it has an eerie, rose-tinted beauty. But Anna has no awareness of this beauty. She is too tired to contemplate anything. She has been through a terrible energy-sapping ordeal. She makes a bed for herself—using the folded material of the parachute—in a cranny, curls up and goes to sleep.

19.

Was it a curse? Or a gift from the gods? Leonardo pondered this question as he studied himself in the mirror. Paula disengaged herself from the rumpled sheets and came to stand beside him. Although she too was devastatingly beautiful he paid her little attention. She caressed his face and chest, kissing his shoulder passionately.

'Come to bed,' she whispered. 'Once more.' The memory of their four bouts the previous evening had left her aching.

'I can't. My love,' he stroked her face tenderly, 'I am late for my training. I must tear myself away.'

'You don't love me!' she pouted.

'How can you say that? My love! My beauty! My beloved. I dedicate my future gold medals to you.'

There was much kissing and fondling and hugging. Many sighs—eager, anguished—as he hurriedly dressed and managed—finally—to extract himself from her embraces.

'Till this evening, carissima!' he called out as he hurried out of the door and down the stairs of the apartment house.

The town was just awakening as he ran down the cobbled streets of the medieval city. The walls of the buildings glistened pink in the blossoming glow of the morning sun.

'Ah! Rose red city!' he thought to himself with a surge of poetic inspiration. 'Half as old as time!' He had heard these words somewhere. Where? It mattered not. He gloried in this early morning moment as he jogged gracefully along the empty streets. But his reveries were interrupted as he had half hoped they would be. A head popped out of a first floor window.

'Leonardo!'

Leonardo looked up and caught sight of the devastatingly beautiful, blonde, blue-eyed Maria.

'Come!' she called and he felt it would be ungallant to refuse. She met him at the doorway and threw her arms around him.

'Come! Alfredo has already gone!'

'Ah Maria! Maria!' he took her face in his hands and gave her a deep, deep kiss.

'I have torn myself away from training just to see you. My beloved. My sweetness,' he lied. And then for the next ten minutes there was only the sound of an intense struggle—the archetypal struggle of Man and Woman seeking to wrench from each other the last drop of exquisite pleasure. But that pleasure having been wrenched he was once again on his feet, dressing himself.

'Stay!' Maria pleaded. 'Don't go!'

He stooped to suck the sweetness of her lips.

'I must go, my beloved,' he said, his limpid eyes beseeching her to understand. 'I must tear myself away!'

'You don't love me!'

Leonardo threw his arms wide in an expression of the most sincere disbelief.

'How can you say that? You are my true love. I dedicate to you my future gold medals.'

Despite her further entreaties, he managed to extricate himself from her arms and flee. Already the sun was higher in the sky and he was late. He ran all the way to the swimming complex where he quickly changed.

'Hey, Leonardo!' His friend and swimming companion, Alfredo, greeted him with a high five.

'How's it going buddy?'

Leonardo refrained from telling him that he had just this minute come from Alfredo's own bed where he had done what Alfredo apparently couldn't do. He understood that to say these things might be hurtful and would put his own friendship with Alfredo at some risk. If Leonardo had a fault it was that he wanted everyone to be happy. He simply could not say no. Instead, he wanted to say something nice, something good. He leant forward and whispered to him:

'I have just this minute come from the bed of the most beautiful woman in the whole city.'

Alfredo laughed.

'Impossible,' he said. 'Because I too have just come from the bed of the most beautiful woman in the whole city. And I am so lucky because I am married to her.'

Leonardo gestured that perhaps Alfredo was right.

How could he argue with him?

'Anyway,' Alfredo said. 'Coach is looking for you!' and laughingly slapped his arm. 'You're in trouble.'

So Leonardo strolled to the coach's office. He found her studying the time sheets. As soon as she saw him she rapped her finger on her wrist watch and then gave that hand signal, a shaking of the cupped hand at waist level that unmistakably says to other Italians that some derisory mocking is going on in the signaler's mind.

'When are you going to take your training seriously?' Her hands had come to rest on her sumptuous hips. Leonardo could not but admire her as his frank gaze unmistakably informed her. She had long tumbling raven hair that cascaded over her shoulders. Her large bosom heaved with her outrage.

'How can you say that?' Leonardo protested.

'Every day you are late. Every day you arrive exhausted.'

'Exhausted? Never! He stepped closer to her and sensed a ripple of some long suppressed emotion animate her flesh.

'Truly, I speak from the heart,' he took another step towards her. 'I can think of nothing else but the Olympics.'

'Nothing?' her hands trembled as she raised them and let them land on the bed of hair on his approaching chest. His lips came down on hers with a fierce passion. She did not resist. Slowly they sank to the floor. Anyone pausing at the door to have a word with the coach was immediately made aware that she had other, urgent, more important, things to attend to right now and that anything that needed to be done was best left till later.

When they were finished, Leonardo made his way back to the pool and dived in. The first fifty lengths were always his favourite. He enjoyed the sense of his body rippling through the water. Each length required a different stroke—crawl down to the end, backstroke back, breaststroke down to the end and butterfly back. On and on. He was so looking forward to the Olympics, enjoyed particularly the thought that the world's cameras would be there taking his image across the world. It would be plastered across the covers of all the magazines. He would be famous. Maybe he would go to Hollywood and become a new Tarzan, a new James Bond, a new ... anything. He was looking forward to, how did they call it, dating? He was looking forward to dating all the Hollywood actresses: Lindsay, Cameron and ... he couldn't remember any other names, all the rest of them. They would be queuing up to date Leonardo.

☙

He was just getting into his stride when he felt someone touch him to get his attention. He stopped swimming and looked up. The swimmer who had touched him pointed to the end of the pool where the coach was standing. She was clearly angry about something. Women! What would the world be like without them? He swam up to her and then took off his goggles and swimming cap so as to attend to her more completely. It was clear there was something wrong. Her face was twisted with fury.

'What is it, carissima?'

'You said you loved me!'

'I do! From the depth of my heart. I dedicate my future gold medals to you.'

'Oh yes?' she screamed, her voice echoing around the pool hall. 'Shouldn't you be dedicating it to her?' She pointed to a beautiful girl who was standing near the entrance, waving to him, trying to get his attention. But it wasn't the girl's beauty that angered the coach. It was the fact that she was obviously five months pregnant.

'You see this?' The coach screamed pointing at a sheet of paper that she was even now tearing into a hundred little pieces.

'This is your Olympic application form. There! Take it! You are finished. Finito.' She drew a finger across her throat and stomped off.

Leonardo, slowly, effortlessly heaved himself out of the pool. For the next ten minutes the air was blue with the sound of their mutual outrage. There was much hand signalling of the type the Italians are famous for. But even Leonardo's immense treasure trove of charm was this time unequal to the task of placating a woman so cruelly scorned.

This had been some time ago. So when the 'L'affare di Rowan Jones' as if was referred to in the Italian press came and went, it also came and took Leonardo with it.

'This Rowan Jones is a good man!' Leonardo declared to Maria, in whose bed he was now able to dally longer now that he was no longer in serious training. 'I will go and see him.'

'But first you will come here,' Maria said and pulled his head unresistingly into the warmth of her capacious bosom.

20.

The heat of the desert sent shivering shocks of shimmering waves shuddering through the shadeless air. It was that kind of day. The camel undulated, ungulatingly, along. Anna rocked back and forwards, feeling more camel sick than she could remember being ever before. Her bum and thighs were badly chafed. An eternity of dunes danced into the dazzling, constantly evaporating distance. She kept looking behind her. For some reason she had got it into her head that she was being followed. But everywhere she looked it was the same—a dance of dizzying, shimmering waves, sand dunes dissolving into yet more sand dunes. Yet the shadow of the sense persisted. Somewhere, somehow, someone was following her. The ungulate under her undulated once more sickeningly. She wanted to vomit but she had already emptied everything in her stomach over the camel's flea-bitten back. 'Are we nearly there yet?' she wanted to cry, did cry, but the camel driver took no notice of her. Perhaps he was deaf. Perhaps the desert winds that were forever blowing deafened those forced to debauch their dire, dreary destinies here. Perhaps. And she looked again behind her to see if she could see who it was that her heart now insisted was following her. But there was nothing there. Just an enervating eternity of ceaseless sand.

21.

The view of the old city of Jerusalem is justly famous, the golden light glinting off the gilded roof, the Garden with its cypress trees. The eternal source of all things imbues the spirit of this city with its spirit. Much has changed over the centuries. Much is undoubtedly as it was from the beginning. Streets once formed continue forever, continue through time to the end of time. Rocks may remain but the buildings they support change and are renewed. So it is that the building we find ourselves looking at is clearly newly built, but the materials of the walls are as old as the hills from which they came. Inside this building is a sports centre and in one room of this centre is a space dedicated to the art of weightlifting.

'For God's sake, Solly! What is your problem?' The speaker, Jacob Rabinowitz, was a large, barrel-chested, bearded man and he spoke in the loud, deep, hectoring voice common to large, barrel-chested bearded men. The man he was speaking to was lying on a bench with a heavy weight suspended above him on a rack. He too was a large, barrel-chested bearded man, with, if anything, even larger muscles than his companion. At the ends of the weight stood two men, also well-muscled, ready to catch it should Solly—or Solomon to us, as we have not known him long enough to be so familiar—lose his grip on it.

'What is there not to understand?' Solomon shouted, equally angry. 'You don't exist. I don't exist. None of us has that right.'

'Touch me, Solomon. Believe me. I exist. I am here. You can see for yourself.'

'You know what I mean. Of course I exist as a man. You think I am mad. But I do not exist as Solomon Abrahams, citizen of the State of Israel. That is the entity that does not exist, that refuses to exist.'

'Do we not have the right? Did we not fight wars? Did we not win?'

'Out of my sight!'

'Are we not here?'

'Do not test me, Satan! Only God can lead us to the Promised Land.'

'But, I repeat, are we not here? Is anything possible without God?'

'Listen to me and listen carefully for this is the last time I will explain what should not need explaining. God did not lead us to Israel. Men did. God did not give us back this land.

Men did. We are here because of an historical accident not because of divine necessity. If God in his wisdom is watching us, he watches us with a hard heart. Man must not assume to do what only God has a right to do. This Israel is not God's Israel. Therefore I refuse to recognize it. Now go! I have said already too much.'

'But Solly ...'

'Are you deaf? Go!' Solomon roared with exasperated rage, gripped the weight and thrust it into the air. Then he let it down slowly over his neck. Then up he thrust it into the air until his arms were straight.

'There!'

The two men helped to guide the weight back onto the rack.

'What do you think?'

'You're good enough to get the silver,' said the young man to Solomon's left with a wink to his companion.

'Pah!' Solomon uttered in disgust. 'If I went, I would get gold!'

The two men raised their eyebrows at each other. Anything was possible. More's the pity he refused to go.

That evening Solomon attended the wedding of his nephew. He stood with a group of men all dressed in traditional black clothes and all bearded. These were the people among whom he felt most comfortable, men with whom he could discuss and dispute on matters of interpretation of the Talmud and the other scriptures. But recently, these discussions had taken on an unpleasant dimension. The lines were clear. On the one side there were those, who, like him, felt no need to defend their stance. What was, was. On the other were those who insinuated seductive reasonings—who simply would not let the business lie. Like the man who was talking now.

'You have a great gift, Solomon.' This was the path of flattery. Many had tried but he was impervious to this approach.

'It is a gift that, with God's help, I have given to myself.'

'Perhaps you can do it for the glory of your people, Solly?'

'And who are my people?'

'The Jews, Solly, the Jews.'

'When there is a Jewish nation invited to take part in the Olympics, then I will gladly go.'

'But there is a Jewish nation, Solly. We are here. Israel.'

'My friend, I have already sworn never to discuss this matter again so let this be the last time. If I could do this thing to honour my family, I would go. To honour my friends and neighbours? Then, too, I would go. To honour all those who share our religion, then yes, why not? I would go. To honour God, of course I would go. But this state of Israel is not God's doing. It is the work of the devil. For that reason I cannot recognize it. And so, gentlemen, following this logic, I cannot go to the Olympics as an official sporting ambassador of a country that for me does not exist. Is that clear? Can we not talk of other things? What does it matter? All is vanity? When I lift a weight, I do not do it so that I can say to myself, I am doing this to win gold medals at the Olympic Games. No. Rather, I say I am able to do this because God has given me the strength to do it, so thank you God. Thank you. Now, has the dancing started?'

'Soon ...'

But a young man had been standing on the edge of the group listening respectfully to the dispute. When Solomon finished talking there was a brief silence.

'Perhaps I have the answer,' he murmured diffidently, pulling a newspaper cutting out of his jacket pocket. He unfolded the piece of paper and handed it to Solomon. Solly's expression went from one of fierce and taut resolve to one as soft and malleable as dough. A tear leaped to his eye and flowed down his cheek. He read to the end, silently mouthing out each word. Then, only then, did he stand up, seeking out the young man. He found him and enveloped him in a crushing hug, almost smothering the lad. Then the music started and his legs started to jig and jerk. He let the man go and broke into the most feverish and joyful dancing.

22.

'Indeed!' Rowan said, jabbing his point into the air. He had found another ear to bend. An eager ear that hung on every movement of his hand. 'It is a vital part of the Olympic mission to, and I quote: 'to encourage and support the development of sport for all.' For all! Do you understand what that means? That means for everyone. Every single person on this planet. No exceptions!'

His companion growled and waited for Rowan to throw something into the air that he could fetch.

23.

The two fighters circled each other cautiously. Their movements were like a synchronized dance. The second—the millisecond!—that one moved, the other responded. So fast was the response it was rarely clear who had initiated and who had responded. It was as if they were bound together by an invisible force. As indeed they were.

Each had a black belt round his white jacket. Each had a black mole on the left cheek. Yoshi and Toshi. When they were born the second baby skidded out so fast after the first that they got mixed up and confused so no-one ever knew which of them was the elder. They had competed hard with each other ever since. They were two identical halves to one turbulent whole. Together they fought hammer and tongs; separated, for whatever reason, they became listless, filled with a vacant yearning. Coming together again after a time apart, like two equal and opposite particles, they collided explosively. Toshi and Yoshi.

Even Mum could not tell them apart and had long ago given up trying. Dad, sadly, was dead. But it was Dad who had had the intuition to enrol them on a martial arts course when they were both only four years old. He was fed up with their constant bickering and scrapping and hoped to teach them discipline. And they did learn the discipline but they had also learned the skills that fighters need and because they were so unusual they had early on caught the eye of the school bullies. So they quickly agreed, even without speaking to each other—they had long known that they shared each other's thoughts—that much as they would dearly love to scrap with each other, they would put that fight on hold till they had dealt with the external threat. And there had been no end to these external threats.

Nobu had been the first. A school bully of the classical mould. Backed up by his cronies, he picked on the weak and pocketed their lunch money. But Yoshi and Toshi weren't going to play that game, even though Nobu was six years older than them. One day, early on in their school career, they had found themselves cornered at one end of a corridor by Nobu and three pimply thugs. Toshi and Yoshi had simply shrugged at each other and gone on the offensive. By this time they were highly skilled in the ways of judo and karate. They mixed one with the other. Nobu was soon limping away and his acolytes were left wondering if they had better switch their allegiances. And so it went on. One bully after another. From the school playground it went out into the streets. The local Yakuza thugs soon found good reasons for leaving them alone. When it came to bruising encounters it was usually the opponents who were left bruised.

Year after year, competition after competition, nothing could separate them. Too often they would meet as finalists and too often the judges would realize there was nothing between them in skill or in fortitude or even in cunningness of strategy. And of course they understood each other. And usually this was recognized by the judges and the result would be called a draw. They would both be awarded the gold medal, or the cup, or whatever it was that they were competing for. But then came the problem.

'I'm sorry boys,' Coach had said one day. 'The nobs upstairs say only one of you can go. They say you're identical so the one who goes will be fighting for the other one. It doesn't matter which one. It's your choice.'

Yoshi and Toshi had looked at each other uncomprehendingly. Toshi and Yoshi then both asked themselves: 'Why bother?' Yoshi and Toshi both rejected the call to be reasonable. The nobs proved to be equally recalcitrant and dug themselves in. It became a matter of face. There were attempts to mediate the difference but they came to nothing. And, in the end, the officials became so exasperated they banned the two young men from taking part in any competition within their jurisdiction, which meant all competitions, which meant they couldn't fight anyone else, which meant they had to fight each other, which was all they had ever really wanted to do anyway. Though a gold medal to place on Dad's grave stone would have been only right and proper.

So now they were circling each other looking for that blind spot that kept on eluding them. The minute one saw an opening, the other closed it. Then the door to the gym banged open and shut as Coach bustled in. Toshi and Yoshi immediately stopped the bout and bowed to each other, before turning to him.

'Sorry boys,' Coach said. They could see he was in tears. 'I've been told I can't coach you any more or I'll lose my license.'

They patted him on the back.

'We understand,' they told him. He had been a tough coach but they admired him for that, and because he had been scrupulously fair and even handed with them. He was the nearest thing to a father figure that they had.

'That means you can't even fight here on these premises!' Coach was red-faced with his mortification. He had grown to love the two boys as if they were his own sons. But now? Now, the bastards upstairs were forcing him to turn them out on the street. No other gym would touch them. Their careers were over. Even if they went to another city. They were too well known. If they wanted to continue fighting then it would have to be in another country. He had contacts in Korea. Maybe ...? He watched the two boys sag a little, as they slumped under the weight of what he was telling them. He did not judge them. He understood. The impact was too much for anyone to comprehend. And he himself was a coward. If he had any balls, he told himself, he would cut his links too. Go independent. But it wasn't possible. He'd be closed down.

He wouldn't be allowed to coach. The authorities were hand in glove with each other. He was too old to learn another trade. He had to knuckle under. If only the boys had been more sensible! He thought, trying to shift the blame to them. But he understood their point of view too. And so the thoughts swirled in his brain, round and round.

'Come,' he said putting his arm around their shoulders. 'We will have one last dinner together to celebrate the good times.'

Why not? They shrugged. It wasn't Coach's fault. They would treat him. And then ...? The future looked too bleak. They blocked it out. They would think about that tomorrow.

'I don't know if this will interest you,' Coach said as he pulled a newspaper cutting out of his pocket.

'We'll read it tomorrow,' Toshi said, or was it Yoshi? 'Tonight, let's get completely drunk.'

'That's the spirit!' Coach said and slapped them both on the back.

24.

From the desert to the mountains. From the mountains down to the sea. From the sea along the coast. Wherever Anna went the feeling that she was being followed stayed with her. They knew where she was. Of this she was certain. And now she was forced to leave these remote spaces. Ahead of her lay the cities of Europe. Each step that took her nearer to London was becoming more weighted with threat. But what choice did she have? She carried with her dangerous knowledge. They would do anything to stop her. For the moment she was one step ahead. But for how much longer?

25.

There was a smack of leather against leather followed by a spatter of sweat and a grunt. Again the smack. And again the grunt.

The two boxers shuffled apart for a moment before the one in the red pants began again to jog and bounce from side to side with menace. The other raised a hand.

'Stop! Enough!'

'Put your hands up and defend yourself.' The other growled.

'Let's take a break.'

'Call yourself a fighter?'

'Basta! We've been at it an hour already.'

The fighter in the blue pants took the head protector off and shook her dark curly hair. Her skin was an olive complexion. The other fighter pulled off her gloves in disgust and hurled them to the floor. Then she also took off her head protector. She was dark, this one, dark as her slave forebears—dark as grey slate—but a beauty if you discounted the slightly thickened lips where she had taken too many blows. There was a classical symmetry to her features. And there was drama too in her face. It was fortunate that she had never had her nose broken.

'Bravo!' shouted an old man ironically and began a slow clap. He was seated on a bench ten feet away from the ring but there was no-one else in the boxing gym to impede his view.

'Ah shaddup!' both fighters gestured disgustedly in his direction as they approached each other and hugged. Then they kissed tenderly for a long moment before once again breaking apart.

'Hayee!!!!' shrieked the old man in delight but no-one took any notice of him.

'Finished already?' The well dressed , rather stocky man had wondered over from the far side of the gym where he had been putting two young fighters through their paces.

'Ay! Carmen has no energy any more. She's forgotten how to fight,' the dark one said.

Carmen laughed, her thick black eyebrows raised mockingly.

'Since Julia left her, Leona just wants to fight. She needs another lover.'

'Not you?'

'Not me! I'm just a temporary plaything. I'm a married woman with kids. She needs a serious lover.'

'Is that true Leona?' the man asked. 'That you fight better when you don't have a lover?'

'What's it to you?'

'I have two young fighters. They'd have enough energy for you.' He laughed. 'You'd soon be begging them to stop.'

They all laughed at this, Leona most of all.

'Ayiihh! I would eat them both for breakfast.'

She walked over to a bench, picked up a skipping rope and started to skip.

'Why do you train so hard?'

'Chico, it is simple. So simple even you might understand. If I don't keep fit then I can't fight. If I don't fight, I'm not in the running for the team. If I am not selected, then they won't put me on a plane and fly me across the Atlantic Ocean to London, to the Olympic Games. I might as well go home and beat the shit out of my cat.'

'So, you're serious about the Olympics?'

'Sure I'm serious. Why wouldn't I be?'

'You could make it a certainty.'

'How?'

'I have something that can make your muscles grow faster.'

Leona laughed dismissively: 'Sure.'

'I'm serious. Look at my boys.' He pointed to the far end of the gym where the two lads were still pummelling each other. 'Have you seen how they've grown stronger in the last six months?'

Leona's face twisted and spat on the floor.

'You disgust me.'

'What did you say?' the man was no longer affable.

'You heard.'

'You forget that I have influence.'

Carmen saw what was happening and tried to intervene.

'Leona, come. Let's go and have a coffee.'

Leona just waved her away and pointed her finger at the man.

'Chico, you listen to me. If I am selected it will be an honest selection. That is all I have to say.'

The man laughed.

'Don't hold your breath. Uncle Pedro will make sure you have no chance. All I have to do is drop the word' He chuckled. 'In fact, I'm seeing him this evening. Let's see. Is your brother still running drugs in the sierra?'

Leona spat again.

'My brother has more principles in his little finger than you will ever have.'

'So,' the man dropped his cigarette on the floor and

stood on it. 'He is a left wing revolutionary. If anything that is even worse than a drug smuggler. So you are even more suspect. How can the government send you abroad as an ambassador, a sports ambassador? And of course there is the matter of your sexual preferences.'

'Ah, stick it up your ass!'

'So, all of this training is a waste of time.' Chico continued to mock.

'Get in the ring with me and I'll show you.'

'I don't fight women.'

'That's not what I've heard,' Leona retorted. 'From the whores in the harbour.'

The man's face darkened with anger.

'One day, ...' He left the words hanging there so that everyone could weigh up the level of threat they contained. Everyone knew that Chico's uncle Pedro was an important man. Among other things he was Chairman of the national Olympic executive. He also owned the local first division football team, the local television station, and the leading newspaper. If rumours were to be believed, he also owned the local police force and the worker's union. He controlled the flow of drugs that came from the jungle laboratories. He controlled the amount of firearms that were available to the local street gangs. In short, he controlled just about everything. And if he didn't think that Leona Sanchez-Martinez should represent her country at the Olympics then it was a simple matter for him to make sure she didn't. But Leona was not the kind of person to listen to reasons of this sort. Leona had long since stopped listening to the logic of force.

'One day?' she repeated. Leona had stopped skipping. She walked up to him and put her face in his. 'One day?' They stood eyeball to eyeball neither backing down.

Carmen again tried to intervene.

'Come on. Let's go and have a coffee.'

But Leona shook her off. She was about an inch taller than Chico and she made that inch count.

'I may not have any balls but I still have more than you.' She growled.

Chico could not let this go. He whipped a knife out of his jacket pocket but before he had a chance to wield it a fist smashed into his nose, followed almost immediately by one to the side of his head. Within a few seconds he was lying on the floor. Either she'd knocked him unconscious or he was doing a good job of pretending.

'Come on!' Carmen tugged at Leona's arm.

'Bastard!' Leona aimed a kick at his groin that only half connected. 'I should kill you.'

The two young boxers came over rather shyly to defend their coach.

'Does he give you drugs?' Leona asked. They nodded.

'He gives us injections,' the taller one said

'He says it is vitamins,' said the other and rubbed his nose with his glove.

Leona shook her head. She knew it was no good. These kids had no future except maybe they were good at boxing. If the boss said take drugs they'd take them. Why not? What else did they have going for them?

'Come Leona, get your stuff. You can't come back here or he'll kill you.' Carmen tugged on her arm. Leona nodded. She knew Carmen was right. Maybe it was time to head for the hills, to join her brother in the struggle. But that too was a lost cause. She felt weighed down by the immense burden of hopelessness. Surely there must be something else she could do. There must be some other route to making her dreams come true. She went to her locker and cleaned it out. She would not be coming back here any time soon. Why was the world so full of assholes? Chico was sitting up rubbing his jaw when they left the gym.

Weeks passed and it rained forever and she felt so alone. Mould spread along the wall of the kitchen. The gutters leaked. The tin roof failed to keep the water out. The television either did not work or was not worth watching. But except when she had to—to get the food in, not so much for herself but for her little cat—she didn't go out. She stared at the sheets of rain. Hopelessness settled on her. With boxing she was something—not to the world maybe, but to herself. Without boxing she was nothing. With boxing there was reason and hope. Without? Nada. Menos que nada, less than nothing. So she fed the cat and stared blankly at the plummeting sacs of tropical rain. One day the money would run out and she would starve to death. She didn't care. There was no longer any reason to continue this thing called life. And so her solitary days passed, one after the other. The sun rose. The sun fell. What did she care?.

Then, one day, an envelope was pushed under her front door. Inside there was only a paper cutting. It was an article on the Olympics. She wanted to tear it to pieces and would have done if there hadn't been a paragraph circled in ink. It discussed the idealism of a Welsh poet called Rowan Jones. She read it first out of duty, then read and re-read it again, bewildered that such heroism and altruism were possible in this wretched life. So! She thought. This Jones hombre better have some cojones.

Then she picked up the phone and let it ring until it was finally answered.

'Carmen?'

'Yes, Leona. What is it?'

'You need to find some money for me. I need to fly to London.'

'London?'

'Yes, I'm going to visit a poet in Wales.'

Carmen smiled. It was she who had slipped the envelope under the door so she understood.

'I have the money for you. You don't even have to sleep with me to get it.'

Leona laughed.

'Sleep? There will be no sleeping! I promise you that.'

Part Three

1.

It has been a long journey. We last met Mad Mike, Brother-of-the-ocean-turtle, sculling across the calm azure waters of a distant atoll unknown to the world, a place of paradisal beauty. Now he was sculling on the choppier, heaving green-grey waters of the Irish Sea. Had he sculled across oceans? Not a bit of it. He had hitched a lift first on an inter-island tramp ship—for how long would there still be boats plying these distant waters, the empty oceanic quarter of the planet?—then, after going the rounds of his far flung family, twisting arms, making bets on arm wrestling and posing for nearly nude photographs at a Gay Parade, he had raised the cash to fly business class to Heathrow. From there he went to see his old mate Steve Redgrave—Sir Steve, he now styled himself. How long would he get away with that? Sir Steve fitted him out with a spare scull he had in the garage. All he needed now was to try it out. They took it to a lake where they both had fun cracking up and down seeing how fast they could make the thing move. Steve showed he wasn't a spent force by any means. But Mad Mike wasn't sold on all this fresh water. It didn't seem natural to him. The buoyancy just wasn't the same. Just wasn't right somehow. So Steve dropped him off at a little harbour in Wales that really just couldn't have been cuter.

'You sure you're going to be all right?' Sir Steve asked.

'Oh yeah. I've got to thank you, Steve. You've been a real heads up mate. But I'm going to be all right, I reckon. The poet geezer lives just round here somewhere. I'm just going to have a quick scull in the sea, see how it goes, then I'll be off to pay my respects to the man and check out the big picture.'

'Well, Turtle,'—that was the name that Steve called him—'If you need any more help just get on the blower.'

Mad Mike gave him a big thumbs up. A moment later he was sculling out to sea. This was a lot better he thought. He could taste the salt of the water and the stink of seaweed titillated his nostrils. He scooped a handful of water into his mouth to savour it. Oh yes! He'd been away from the sea for a good ten days now and he had missed it. Something was different, though, but it took him a while to understand it. Then it came to him. It was now after eight in the evening and it was still light. He wasn't used to that. In his part of the world the night fell down with a bang at six o'clock, give or take a few minutes, every night of the year. Nor was he used to this pale pearly light that hung on and on for an hour, two even; a pale light that slowly—so very, very slowly—oranged and crimsoned into night. Hmm. Tempus fugit, he thought. Time waits for no man. He'd best scull himself back to shore and find this poet man.

There was a small beach by the side of the main jetty and Mad Mike hauled the scull on to the sand. But there was a sea wall that was going to make it difficult. He didn't want to leave it on the seaward side. Steve had warned him about the tides. While he was mulling over the problem a large, bearded, barrel-chested man jumped down on to the sand beside him.

'You will want a hand with that.' Not a question.

Mad Mike was surprised. Strangers tended to take one look at the tattoos on his face, and the size of his own impressive physique, and give him a wide berth. But here in front of him was a man who even he would have second thoughts about tangling with. Fortunately the man seemed entirely good natured.

'You are local to this place?' this time it was a question. Mad Mike wondered how to respond. Did he look like he was local? But then again many people belonged even when they didn't look it. And the local people from hereabouts probably did tattoo their faces two thousand years ago. He shook his head with amiable wariness.

'Well, anyway, let's get this boat safe.' With one hand, the man picked up one end of the scull and waited for Mad Mike to pick up the other. Together they heaved it up on to the walkway that skirted the sand.

'Thanks mate. Much appreciated.' Mad Mike extended his hand expecting the other man to give it a crushing shake — the kind of shake that says I'm stronger than you fella and don't forget it — but the grip, though firm, was as light as a lemon tart. The man had confidence in himself. He knew his strength and had nothing to prove to anyone. That much was clear. Not that Mad Mike was too impressed. He had already sized the man up as a weight lifter — lots of static muscle, but not that much flexibility. He himself had less muscle bulk but a great deal more sheer litheness and agility. It would not be a one sided fight if they ever did come to blows. He smiled at himself when he became aware of what he was thinking. Why was it strong men, or rather men who defined themselves and other men by their physical strength, assessed each other like this? Looking into the other man's face he saw the twinkling eyes that suggested he too had asked the same question.

'My name is Solomon,' the man said.

'Mike.'

'Good to meet you, Mike. Now ...' Solomon nodded at the scull. 'This looks serious, no?'

'It's serious.'

'That is what I was thinking.'

Mike waited patiently for him to get to his mental destination.

'And because you are serious, I am thinking that maybe you know the answer to a question.'

'What question is that, mate?'

'There is a Welshman. A poet. He lives near here. He is organizing an alternative Olympics.'

'So I understand.'

'Ah you understand too?'

'Yes. I was just about to ask someone where he lives

'So, you don't know?'

'No. Not right now. But my guess is that we can find out easily enough.'

'Just over the hill. About a mile away.'

Both men turned to look at the new speaker. She had been finishing off a cigarette which she now crushed beneath her boot.

'At least that is what they said in the shop there,' she pointed at a newsagent-cum-post-office-cum-mini-supermarket about fifty yards away, at the bottom of the hill that constituted the main street of the village. 'Why should they lie? Except maybe they don't like my French accent. So maybe it is a joke they play on this funny French woman. What do you think?'

They stood in silence contemplating this possibility. Truly it was a village of great beauty, and the soft evening light accentuated this beauty so that it seemed a little slice of Heaven. How could people brought up in such a place play such mean tricks? It wasn't possible. The two men smiled bashfully for even having considered it and Marguerite, for it is she, gave a shrug as if to say you never know with these completely fou rosbifs. They collected their bags and started to stroll in the indicated direction. They were immediately surrounded by a throng of village girls mobbing a man who exuded a subtle but irresistible masculinity from every pore.

'Will you kiss me?' Breathed one and he gallantly leaned over and gave her a peck on the cheek.

'I don't mean that kind of kiss!'

She grabbed him with both hands round his neck and attached her lips to his.

'And me?' shouted another.

'Don't forget me!' shouted a third.

'What's your secret pal?' Mad Mike asked as Marguerite got into the act, pushing the girls away and planting her own kiss on the man, who was of course Leonardo.

'My God! Did I do that?' Marguerite gasped as she let go and staggered back. 'What came over me? That was a moment of pure bestial animality.' She shook her head in bewilderment. 'And it was fantastique!'

Leonardo looked up and saw Mad Mike standing with Solomon and sizing them up saw that they too were athletes and therefore in a position to help him. He pushed the girls away gently.

'Not so much what you call the harassment! Eh? We can have the fun later, maybe. But now I must go.'

But one girl refused to be disentangled. Gently he took her hands away and placed them by her side.

'Another time, pretty girl.'

'Oi! Who you calling pretty, then?' she spat in disgust.

'I'm no pretty girl.'

Leonardo, surprised at her vehemence, shrugged and retreated. When the girls threatened to pursue him, Mad Mike and Solomon stepped forward and held them off.

'I don't know what you have,' Solomon shook his head from side to side in wonder. 'But maybe you should bottle it and sell it.'

Meanwhile Marguerite was stroking Leonardo's arm in a manner of complete surrender. Mad Mike and Solomon exchanged a look of amused complicity. If either of them had had thoughts regarding Marguerite then they knew enough to know it was a lost cause. Ah well!

'Now, I am looking for the professor of the poetry ...' Leonardo spoke in the sad, gentle, almost despairing patois of his Neapolitan home.

'Aren't we all, mate? Join the queue.'

'The queue?'

He looked around to see if there was a queue. He had heard about the famous English queue.

'You're coming with us,' Marguerite said firmly. Leonardo liked that. He always liked a strong woman. He was a weak man and easily led astray. The trouble was, as he knew from long experience, there were so many strong women. It was impossible to satisfy them all, hard though he tried.

Just then ...

৵

But we must approach this imminent moment from another angle.

Barnaby, the diminutive fencer, the best in all of England, was comfortably ensconced in the back of his pink Rolls Royce. Beside him was a table of oysters, which he was enjoying with noisy gusto. The taste of brine was heavy on his tongue. From time to time he cleansed his palate with a mouthwash of champagne. But he was getting nervous. The street had grown narrower and narrower until they were almost scraping the sides of the fishermen's cottages (fishwives' cottages too!). Cosy little dwellings that seemed to Barnaby to be pleasantly proportioned. But he was growing anxious for the car. It would not be a pleasant experience to be wedged between two houses, completely blocking the street. It would not be appreciated by the local people.

'I say, Perkins. Are you sure this is right?'

'Quite certain, sir.'

'You're sure the satnav hasn't lured us into a cul de sac?'

'It's not far now, sir. Just the other side of this village and over the hill if I'm not mistaken.'

For some reason this remark irritated Barnaby.

'Confound it, Perkins! You are never mistaken. That is one of your most obnoxious habits. To err is human, Perkins. If you don't err, Perkins, what are you? Do you get my drift?'

'I do, sir. I shall endeavour to err.'

'Good.' Barnaby sat back contentedly, with the sense of a job done, a job that needed doing. Taking Perkins down a peg was necessary from time to time. He was relieved to see that the street had widened somewhat.

'However, there may be a problem.' Perkins sounded troubled.

'What problem are we talking about now?'

'The question of erring.' There was a thoughtful pause as he packed the thought in suitable language. 'If I succeed in erring, have I really erred?'

'Not now, Perkins!' Really the man could be intolerable sometimes. 'This is not a time for philosophy. Nor is it a time for erring.'

117

'No sir,' Perkins responded. 'I quite understand.'

It was at that moment that …

❧

But there is a third point of view that needs to be explored before the eventful moment. Ayesha had come from the other end of the village and so entranced was she by the setting sun that hit her full in the face as she turned a corner that she didn't, at first, see the gaggle of girls. Then, when she finally registered their existence, she idly wondered what they were so excited about. That's when she saw Leonardo. Her immediate instinct was to brake but the cobblestones were slicked with the oily wet of the Irish Sea. The bike skidded straight into the front of a stupidly placed pink Rolls Royce that was taking up the whole of the street. Bang went the bike and car as they collided. Ouch went Ayesha as she slapped onto the bonnet of the car and came to rest smeared across the windscreen.

Mad Mike, Solomon, Marguerite and Leonardo all heard the screech of bicycle brakes and the definite thud of a body making contact with a car bonnet. Looking up the main street they could see a pink Rolls Royce with a cyclist sprawled across the front. The doors of the car burst open.

'Perkins! Is she all right?'

'I'm endeavouring to ascertain the facts, sir.'

The body was clearly that of a woman of North African or Middle Eastern origin.

'Ouch!' said the voice attached to the body a second time, more plaintively. 'That was close!'

A small crowd had formed and they watched as she peeled herself off the bonnet and slip back to the ground.

'Is my bike OK?' she asked clutching her ribs.

Sadly, it was clearly not. While the main frame was

untouched, the front forks were bent and the wheel badly buckled.

'I say,' Barnaby drawled. 'I'm so very sorry.'

'It was my fault. I didn't see …! The sun …! That man ….!' She tried to explain what had happened.

'Well, as long as you're not hurt …'

'I'm fine, I think. Just a little ….' she mimed a shiver.

'Of course. Badly shaken. Well, we'll give you a lift to wherever you're going.'

Suddenly, a woman, black and beautiful, materialized and placed a damp piece of red cloth against Ayesha's forehead.

'This will help.'

'Really,' Ayesha protested. 'I'm all right.'

'Don't worry.' The woman smiled. She could have been a model, Ayesha thought, if her lips weren't so puffy. 'You are shaken. I will carry your bags.'

'No, really …' Ayesha wanted to protest but no-one was paying her any attention. Except for the black woman who had such a sweet smile.

'My name is Leona,' she whispered. 'I am your friend.'

All this commotion had percolated throughout the community. Nothing as exciting as this had happened since 1859 when the Reverend Huw Jones had brought God to the village as part of what became known as the Great Revival. Now that had been an occasion and it lasted long in the local memory. First God, then, only one hundred and fifty years later, a pink Rolls Royce. Was there no end to the excitement?

A man's head emerged from the door of the local public house. It was a dark skinned face that had the white moustache of a Guinness on its lips. Kono observed the scene with educated eyes. He had long ago learned that a scene had best be observed at length before he entered it. In this

119

direction lay survival. The threat of a sudden absence of survival was a great educator. He had lived with this threat forever. Kono had also learnt that a man enjoying a glass of beer had a better likelihood of survival than a man going about his business in the street. Or so, at least, it seemed after the second glass of beer. But there were aspects of the scene he was observing that intrigued him. A few words wafted up the hill past him. '… the poet. Rowan Jones …' He drained his glass, set it down carefully on a table, picked up his small bag and joined the throng that was milling round this mirage of pinkness.

'Well,' Barnaby was saying. 'I suppose you'd all best get in.'

And so they did. One after the other. Mad Mike and Solomon, Leonardo and Marguerite, Ayesha and Leona, and Kono. As they were doing so a diminutive Chinese girl sprang from the crowd and did a series of handstands and somersaults up the boot of the car and along the roof, ending on the bonnet.

'Me too!' she said and Perkins waved her in. But before the door could be shut again a strong hand gripped the door frame.

'Y'all wouldn't know where I could find a certain poet of Welsh extraction, a fella by the name of Jones, now would you?'

'Grab a pew,' Barnaby said.

'Grab a what?'

'Join us. Get in. Make yourself comfortable. The more the merrier.'

The man grinned.

'I was hoping you would say that. Don't mind if I do.' He eased himself in with his long bow and case of arrows. He found a tight place beside Marguerite and forced the space wider with a some dexterous movements of his hips until he was nicely wedged in beside her. Marguerite grimaced and tried to turn away from him but he wasn't having any of that.

'The name's Jeremiah,' he said sticking out his hand to be shaken. Slowly and methodically he shook everyone's hand.

'Charmed, I'm sure,' Barnaby said as he found himself squashed into the corner of the back seat of the car.

Once again the car prepared to set off.

'Wait!'

The voice demanded obedience and Perkins once again brought the car to a standstill.

'You will please to take me too,'

For those able to see, there was a man standing in the middle of the road—a man with the oddest metal legs that anyone had ever seen.

'Perhaps you wouldn't mind sitting up front with Perkins,' Barnaby called out. Then, when Karl was seated he instructed Perkins to proceed.

'And go softly on the pedals,' Barnaby called out. 'It's all getting a bit uncomfortable back here.'

But no sooner were the words spoken than Perkins braked hard again.

'What did I say?'

'I'm sorry, sir but there's a man lying across the road.'

There was indeed. Ivan had little grasp of the English language and so everything he wanted had to be expressed in the clearest of mimes. And how could he most clearly signal that he wanted a car to stop? Lie across the road, of course. And if the car didn't stop? What did it matter? He was only a zek. He would be a zek all his life. What did the world care if it had one zek less? But the car did stop. He picked himself up and made a begging gesture, indicating he needed a lift up the hill.

'Put him in the boot!'

Perkins led Ivan to the rear of the car and indicated the boot. Ivan grinned happily and crawled in. When Perkins returned to the driver's seat he saw that there were two identical Japanese men grinning to all and sundry seated on Karl's knees. He shrugged. The more the merrier, he supposed.

Once again they set off and this time there was nothing to impede their passage. Slowly they crested the hill leaving behind that village of immeasurable beauty. And then, a few miles further on, there was a sign in Welsh that Perkins was able to decipher, a sign which pointed the way to the farm where at that very moment Rowan Jones was having an evening of domestic bliss with his dear Bronwyn and the cats and dogs and ducks and hens and rabbits and pigs that they shared the kitchen with.

Even now, the sun still had not set on the scene. In the fading light, the last rays of that precious day, the pink Rolls Royce inched its way along a rutted farm track towards the house.

Rowan and Bronwyn having heard the unfamiliar noise of a car went to their door and opened it. Perkins got out of the car and approached them.

'The great contemporary post-modernist Welsh poet, Rowan Jones, I presume,' he said holding out his hand. Rowan Jones reflexively took the proffered hand and shook it.

'Post-modernist?' he queried.

'Neo-traditionalist?' Perkins offered as a replacement.

'Neo-traditionalist?' Rowan pondered the new option. 'Oh yes, I do like that. Mind if I use it?'

'I would be honoured sir. And now, I'd like to introduce you to a few of your fans, admirers, spiritual fellow travellers or should I say ...'

But Rowan Jones was no longer listening. He was

looking in amazement as one by one the athletes extricated themselves from the black hole of the Rolls Royce. Somehow, along the way, they appeared to have picked up the Welsh basketball team who were emerging from the green VW van parked behind the pink Rolls. One by one they all made their way to the house. When they were all finally standing in front of him, Rowan managed to pull himself together. With a gesture of welcome, he said: 'Well, I expect you'd all better come in.'

From somewhere in the deepening dusk came the distinct sound of a cow's fart.

2.

'Escaped!!!' President Osman Osmanakhian glared at the quivering police chief in front of him.

'He ...'

'She!' Osmanakhian murmured tiredly.

'She ...' the police chief hurriedly corrected himself. 'Has been sighted.'

'Where?'

The Police chief walked to a map of Europe and pointed to a number of small cities moving from east towards the west.

'Here ...' he stabbed the map, venting the ferocity that he knew the president would soon be venting on him. 'And here. And here.' If he was going to save himself this was the moment, his opportunity.

'Our spies are everywhere. He ... She won't get far. We will catch her ... and then! Then!' He did his best to sound menacing but it came out more like a bleat. President

Osmanakhian heard this inner bleating and smiled.

'And then?' he taunted the police chief. 'And then, what will you do to my precious Anna?'

The Police Chief knew a trap when he saw one.

'And then ...' He was thoroughly unnerved and his voice weakened even further. 'Then we will await your instructions.'

Osmanakhian suddenly had a thought. He looked at the map with interest.

'You say here? ... and then here? .... And then here?'

'That's right.'

Osmanakhian wheeled round.

'Does this not tell you something?'

'Yes sir! It tells me we will catch her as soon as she ...'

'Dolt!' Osmanakhian screamed the word as he slapped the man's head hard. 'Why am I surrounded by dolts? Don't you see the obvious?'

The police chief was now completely at a loss. Shaking he tried to rescue himself but didn't know how.

'It tells me we have seen,' he paused to get it right, 'her. That we are only one step behind ...'

Osmanakhian interrupted again slapping his empty gloves feebly across the man's face.

'Stop your blathering.'

He stabbed the map with a wooden pointer, and continued stabbing as he punctuated his words. 'Look! ... She is headed in this direction .... So, where is she going? .... If she continues in this direction she will come to .... Oh!' he pretended to be surprised. 'England!' He laughed mockingly again. 'Let me see, now. This England. What is happening there? Oh yes! What a surprise. The Olympic Games. Our little Anna is going to the Olympic Games.' He looked round and was slightly disappointed to find that the only audience for this piece of spectacular deduction was the very deflated, utterly terrified, Chief of Police. He turned his back on the man so that he could more effectively enjoy a moment of quiet, yet dramatic, reflection: 'So, Anna! That's how you want to play this game? Then I will let you succeed.'

He whirled round again to face the police chief.

'Nothing! Do you hear me? Nothing! You will do nothing to stop Anna. On the contrary, you will instead do everything you can to help her get there.' His eyes glazed as he sank into a reverie. 'And I too will be there. Oh Anna. It will be like old times. You and me! Oh what glory we will bring to Transcaucasia!'

Then recollecting himself he glared at the police chief.

'Go! Do not disturb me! I have important things to do. Go! Go!'

The Police Chief didn't need to be told four times. He turned and jogged as fast as he could out of the presidential presence.

୬

When he was sure he was alone, Osmanakhian went behind a handily placed screen and emerged seconds later dressed as a dominatrix with a whip in his hand. He moved in a sensual, snake like manner around the room. There was a definite hiss in the atmosphere as he prowled to the window and back, cracking his whip. From the far end of the room there was a click as the door began to open. In a flash Osmanakhian had flung himself back behind the screen and by the time his dear wife had fully entered the room he was once again dressed as a president should be—red sash and all.

The first lady was accompanied, this time, by a little Chihuahua. Osmanakhian was ecstatic as he tickled the little creature.

'Ah there you are my little wittle, messy poo-poo. And

how is my teeny-weeny widdler-piddler then?'

It was clear the Presidential Ornament had decided on an adventure in the outside world and if he had any sense he should just shut up and go along with it. But before he handed himself over entirely to her schemes he let one thought rise from the very depths of his being and bubble to the surface.

'Oh Anna. We will all go to London, to the Olympic Games. And there we will show them. You will show them what you can do. And I will show them what kind of man Osman Osmanakhian is. Oh yes! They will see!'

3.

Venice. The Piazza San Marco. The Ponte dei Sospiri. The narrow streets. Anna is bewildered and bewitched. Behind her it seems there is the smack of shoes following her every move—yet every time she looks around there is no-one to be seen. These invisible presences urge her on but she can never escape. Once she went on a run through narrow alleys, running wildly, in any direction, getting hopelessly lost. But although she could lose herself, she never seemed to lose these invisible followers. Were they just echoes? Was she trying to escape from herself? She had almost convinced herself it was so when …. It was like this, clattering across a sunlit square, Anna dived down a dark alley only to find herself suddenly trapped in a huddle of men coming the other way. She was trampled to the ground. The men slapped her and grabbed her bag.

'Wait!' she cried, as they ran off, leaving her penniless, without papers. She had come to the end, it seemed. Her quixotic adventure to expose Osmanakhian's evil scheme had come to nothing.

She got to her knees and then staggered to her feet. Her face was a mess. Her make-up badly smeared by dirt and tears. Her clothes were torn. Who could she turn to? As she was pondering these thoughts a man came towards her. She backed away from him afraid he had come to do her more harm. Instead, as he passed, he slapped a brown envelope into her arms. By the time she understood what had happened he had gone round the corner. She looked at the brown envelope and then tentatively untied the string and opened it. Inside she found a large bundle of Euros and a passport—a passport with her name and her photograph. A passport filled with all the visas a Transcaucasian citizen would need to traverse Europe. She ran to the corner but the stranger had long since disappeared. What was going on? Who was her mysterious backer? Clearly this was all intended for her but why? How? She hardly knew what questions to ask. All she knew was that she had money to spend, a face that needed fixing up and a wardrobe that needed extending. Milan would be her next port of call. Then Paris. Then …. Yes, perhaps, then London. She would see. It was possible her plans might change. Having money to spend always had that affect on her.

4.

B ronwyn was troubled by something. This was obvious to all the animals in the kitchen. And if Bronwyn was troubled so were they. She sat at the dining table with bills and bank statements spread out in front of her and sighed. The sighs came reluctantly for she was not the sad and sighing type. None of the animals could remember seeing her sigh like this before. Why was she so sad? Of course they all wanted to cheer her up. The cats came up to her and pressed themselves against her legs. The dogs looked up at her with floppy-tongued, pantings and playful eyes that said, let's go outside and we'll chase all the balls you care to throw. The rabbits hopped on to the table top and let the quivering of their noses express their most deeply felt anxieties. The hens were edgy. The pigs were restless. Something was up. Finally, Bronwyn penned a note and gave it to the duck to deliver.

The duck waddled out of the back door and across the farm yard where she had to take care not to be trampled on. The Welsh national basketball team had set up hoops and were using the yard as their practice basketball court. To any impartial observer it was clear that a great deal of practice was needed but that on its own, no amount of practice was likely to improve the prospects of the team. Skirting the edge of this makeshift court, the duck came to a stretch of grass where a very short man was fencing with a taller man.

'Damn it, Perkins, that's the third time in a row that you've got through my defences. I thought you said you couldn't fence.'

'Sorry, sir. It won't happen again.'

'That's not the point, Perkins, as you very well know. Now, en garde.'

The clash and counter clash of foils continued for the three minutes that it took the duck to skirt the fencers.

'Dash it, Perkins. Confound it. You make it jolly hard to land a blow. I attack, you counter attack. I riposte. You feint.'

'I do what I can, sir.'

'Where did you learn to fight like this?'

'I've been observing your matches over the years with

great interest.'

'En garde!' Barnaby called out with just the slightest touch of tetchiness in his voice.

The duck waddled on leaving the men to their bickering. Next she passed a barn, where, if she had looked in, she would have seen a diminutive Chinese acrobat walking across a beam high above a bale of hay. This was her safety net, so to speak, in case she slipped and fell while doing one of her handstands, somersaults, back flips and whatever else it is that acrobats do on a beam. At one end of the barn was a large bearded man lifting various items of farm equipment. From time to time Solomon would shout.

'Come, pretty girl.'

And Jade would interrupt what she was doing to see what he required of her.

'Stand on this pole!' he ordered.

Jade stood on the pole while he, seemingly effortlessly raised and lowered it slowly and evenly. Once she had got used to the rhythm of his movements she would then do her splits and headstands while he continued to raise and lower the pole. It seemed to benefit both of them. For him, she added weight to the pole, while he gave her something more challenging to achieve.

But the duck did not stop to look in the barn so saw none of this. Nor did she see into the neighbouring field where Karl, Kono, Ayesha and Ivan raced each other up and down the steep slope. If it might seem that Ivan had an unfair advantage, having as he did a horse to do his running for him, it had been decided between them that Ivan had to do three lengths of the field to every two that Ayesha did on her bicycle (which had been repaired), and which, to win, they had to do before Karl and Kono ran a single length. And of course they could never agree on the result so, after resting a while, they would have to do it all over again. Keeping an eye on things—but particularly keeping an eye on Ayesha—was Leona who had marked out the corner of this field as her exercise area. A punch bag had been suspended from the branch of a large oak and she spent hours at a time pummelling it.

The truth was she was jealous. It was clear to her that Ayesha's eyes had a tendency to glisten more limpidly when Karl was around. But self-knowledge is vital to a fighter if they are to win their fights. It is not enough for them to know their strengths and their opponent's strengths. They must understand the weaknesses too. They must, in particular, know their own weaknesses. Leona understood that she was jealous. In this way she was able to interpret it and keep it under control. For now. But just let Karl abuse the situation and artificial legs or no, he would feel the force of her fist in his face.

❧

The duck's path skirted the top of a cliff. Far below, if the duck had been interested enough to look, she would have seen a small pod of dolphins frolicking playfully in the flat calmness of the silvery sea. Wishing he could swim with them was Leonardo who was in the same sea looking out for them. To share the water of this bay with such magnificent creatures was a privilege, a dream come true. The butterfly was his favourite stroke and he took the movements of the dolphins as his model. Such grace. Such beauty. But Leonardo did not have the luxury of time to watch and admire these beautiful beasts. Behind him there was a school of schoolgirls swimming as fast as they could trying to catch up with him. All the feelings he had for the dolphins, they had for him.

A little further out to sea, a scull was streaking across the glistening, smooth surface.

'Hey!' Leonardo shouted. 'Wait for me!' And he too did a spurt. But he could not hope to catch up with Mad Mike's ferociously hard strokes and the scull slid further and further away. And the dolphins continued to frolic, always just out of reach. And the girls behind him moaned as once again the gap between them and their objective widened.

But the duck did not see any of this. The duck had a mission. She waddled up the last stretch of path, past the mat where the two identical Japanese men were wrestling with each other, to the large greenhouse and rapped on a pane of glass with her beak.

5.

Despite herself, Marguerite had enjoyed this last week. The defensive shields that the athletes had created around themselves protectively had started to dissolve. The sing-alongs organized by the basketball team helped a lot. Then Solomon for all his burly seriousness liked nothing better than to bellow in laughter at the silly jokes he himself told. Like: 'did you hear the one about the Jewish princess who got married? She and her husband had a wonderful honeymoon. They were so happy. And then they came home and he started to use terrible language, what you call four letter words, yes? Oy! Such language she never before heard. She phoned her mother and told her everything. "What are these terrible four letter words he is using?" her mother asked. "He is using all of them," her daughter complained. "Cook, wash, iron ...!" And he would collapse in laughter while the others round the table would look at each other

131

wondering when he would get to the funny bit.

Seeing that that joke had not quite worked he had embarked on another: 'A man was driving along when a police car comes along and makes him stop. The policeman says to him "You are Mister So and So?" He says, "Yes, that's right." And the policeman says. "I'm afraid I have some bad news for you. Your wife fell out of your car two miles back and was killed." "Oh!" he says. "Thank God for that! I thought I was deaf!" Solomon would stare around him. "Thought he was deaf!" he laughed, repeating the punch line in the hope it would be funny second time round. Marguerite smiled at the memory of his incomprehension.

And Bronwyn, poor dear Bronwyn. Such a sweet and pure soul! She had beamed round the room in that sweet pure way she had and said: 'Let's all tell a joke from our own country!' And Ivan had cracked open his ugly face and laughed. 'Here is Russian joke. Handsome man, young army officer, is walking with beautiful girl near river. The girl sees swan, you know, big beautiful white bird and she says to the man: "Isn't the swan such a beautiful bird. I would so much like to be a swan, wouldn't you?" Here Ivan got a laugh for his impersonation of the girl fluttering her eyelashes at the handsome man. 'And the handsome man looks at the girl. He thinks she is crazy. "What?" He asks. "You want to have your naked ass in the cold water all day long?"' Marguerite had seen Jade put her hand flat in front of her face as she laughed. 'What about Chinese jokes?' she'd asked but Jade had just tittered and shaken her head. Nor had anyone else. Except Mad Mike who had some incomprehensible joke about Australians, New Zealanders, sheep and kangaroos. No-one laughed. She supposed it was just an aggressive sexual insult. Men! As for her, she never told jokes so she didn't know any. What was the point of jokes? Such silly things!

Marguerite was remembering all this as she ran through the woods. It was a beautiful trail. Here and there a tree lay across the path and she took the opportunity to hurdle these obstacles. The dirt was dry underfoot. The infamous English weather seemed to have softened. It had not rained once since their arrival. And she was alone! These comrades were friendly enough but what after all did she have in common with them except the desire to excel. She had a mind. She had thoughts. What did these others have besides muscle and commitment? And the Middle Eastern girl, Ayesha. What had she said? Not one word all week! Such a terribly shy girl. It was good to be away from them. It was particularly good to feel her legs working. A pity she would not be able to show off in front of the crowds at the games themselves. But, tant pis, so much the worse for the games!

Her thoughts along these and other lines were suddenly interrupted. At first she thought she had stepped into a hole and was fearful she might twist or break her ankle but the sudden constriction round her leg turned out to be a rope and before she was able to comprehend what was happening she found herself hurtling up into the canopy of the forest. After bouncing up and down a while she came to rest some thirty feet above the ground dangling from a length of rope. Some idiot had set a trap and she had walked into it.

'There's a sucker born every minute.' Said a voice that she recognized straight away.

Marguerite twisted round till she caught sight of him sitting on a thick branch about ten feet from where she was dangling. Jeremiah was whittling a twig with a mean looking knife. How he had managed to get it through customs she didn't know.

'What do you mean sucker? You crazy, dumb, American asshole.'

'Hey! Them's strong words coming from a cheese-eating surrender monkey!'

'How did a Neanderthal like you get loose?'

Jeremiah grinned

'If you're not careful I just might leave you hanging there all night. That would be something, eh?' He chuckled. Marguerite decided the joke had gone on long enough. She used her stomach muscles to bend herself upwards sufficiently to enable her to get a hold first of her legs then of the rope itself. She then hauled herself up the rope to the branch. Despite himself, Jeremiah was impressed.

'You will regret this,' she muttered grimly. Jeremiah decided that perhaps he had gone too far and he would be best advised to make amends.

'Whoah! Hold up. It was a mistake.'

He went to help her and she let him pull her the last few feet on to the branch.

'I really, hand on heart, did not intend for you to get caught in this trap. I do apologise and I sure hope you didn't hurt yourself any. Thing is, I was hunting deer.'

'Deer?'

'We need the meat. We all need the meat.'

'There is meat at every meal.'

'How long do you think our poet friend can afford to go on feeding us all?'

'Ah!'

The truth was Marguerite was suddenly embarrassed. It had never occurred to her to think about the provisions but she could see immediately Jeremiah was right. Rowan and Bronwyn couldn't be expected to go on feeding them indefinitely. They were all being very selfish. This was something they needed to discuss. So irritating that it was this half-educated jungle man who saw this simple truth.

'Now put your arms round my neck,' he told her.

'Touch you?' she could not stop herself from grimacing. 'I'd rather ...'

'How do you think you're going to get down?'

'I ...'

She looked around. Jeremiah was holding on to a rope that was laced through a mountaineering clasp at his waist.

'Like I say. Lessen you want to stay up here all night you'd best grab hold of me and hold on tight.'

Marguerite saw she had no choice in the matter and put her arms round his neck, while she felt his hand pat her bottom appreciatively before clasping it tightly. It had been a long time since her bottom had been so casually patted with impunity, let alone clasped with a grip that claimed ownership. But she had no time to dwell on that as suddenly they were airborne, sailing through the air and, before she knew it, they had landed—so lightly she hardly felt a bump.

'You can let go now.' Jeremiah said with a smile and she hurriedly complied.

He turned away from her and busied himself re-setting the trap.

'I guess you'd best be advised to find another track to run along,' he said over his shoulder.

'How do you know there are deer here anyway?' she asked, dusting herself down.

He looked at her in amazement.

'You don't smell them on the wind? You don't hear them?' he leered so she knew he was mocking her. 'You don't see the droppings?'

Marguerite was abashed at his ease in this place, this woodland, which she had taken simply as a backdrop to her

135

mood but which was for him a living, breathing presence, requiring so much knowledge, so many skills. She felt awkward, as if stranded on some strange shore. Jeremiah was now so involved in his work that she might as well not be there so she turned and started to jog back the way she had come.

'He is not too sophisticated,' she thought to herself as she settled once again into her rhythm. 'But ...' she resisted the thought for a moment, resisted it strenuously. However, it refused to go away and eventually she had to face it 'But,' she sighed. 'He intrigues me.'

6.

Rowan had been mulling over his thoughts with the carp when he heard the rap of the duck's beak on the glass pane. He opened the door and extracted the note from his beak. It was a summons to attend to Bronwyn. As the duck waddled back towards the farmhouse, Rowan, with some foreboding, followed along behind. So it was that, his eyes firmly fixed on his wellington boots, he too did not see the frolicsome dolphins in the silvery sea; did not see Ivan and Ayesha racing horse and bicycle along the side of a field; did not even see Solomon turning a barrel while Jade kept her balance on top of it. So deep were his forebodings that he did not hear Barnaby exclaim in exasperation.

'Confound it, Perkins! Not again!'

Nor did he see the single tall Welsh basketball player dribble single-handedly past the opposition team and slam the ball through the hoop. A makeshift scoreboard turned, recording that the score now stood at 596-0.

At the back door of the farmhouse, Rowan took off his boots and made his way into the kitchen. Bronwyn looked up from where she was sitting, the table in front of her covered in bills.

'I don't know what we're going to do?'

'How do you mean, love?' Rowan was all sad-eyed sympathy. There was nothing so hateful as seeing his dearest beloved Bronwyn upset. She was the concrete of his foundations, the roots of the tree of his being, the … well, you get the drift.

'We just can't go on feeding so many people!'

'Well, we've got to try. They've got nowhere else to go.'

'Well, they've got homes, don't they? Why don't they just go home?'

'Home?'

'There's nothing for them to do here.'

'How do you mean, love?'

'Well, they're not taking part in the Olympics.'

'Ah yes!' Rowan scratched his head. 'I'm working on that.'

'No, you're not. You're just sitting beside your lotus pool doing nothing.'

'Well, being a poet …'

'But you're supposed to be organizing a fringe Olympics or something. But you haven't made one telephone call yet. You've done nothing at all.'

'Ah yes, well …'

'So, they've all had a nice holiday at our expense. Now, it's time for them to go home.'

'Oh no! That wouldn't be right.' Rowan put on the most appealing expression he knew, involving a deep furrowing of his forehead. 'Anyway, love, some of them don't have a home they can go back to.'

Bronwyn stood up and towering over Rowan put her hands on his shoulder.

'But how can we go on feeding them?'

'Oh something will turn up,' Rowan said. Though what that might be he had no idea. However, as it turned out, he didn't have to wait long to find out. At that moment the door opened and in came a man carrying a dead deer.

'Here's a little something for dinner,' Jeremiah said, throwing the animal on the ground. He stood back, the better to see the pleasure he was sure would soon radiate in all directions. But Rowan and Bronwyn just stood there, white faced, open mouthed, in complete shock.

'Oh dear! Oh dear!' Bronwyn murmured.

Rowan was a little slower on the uptake, slower to draw the obvious conclusions, more fearful of them.

'Where on earth did you get that?'

'Over in the woods yonder.' He indicated with his thumb the direction he had just come from.

'Lord Haverford's estate!' Bronwyn breathed with terror. Rowan nodded.

'The gamekeeper will be on to us.'

'Gamekeeper?' This was a new word for Jeremiah but its meaning was clear.

'You mean this here deer ain't wild?'

'Oh God no! It belongs to Lord Haverford.'

'It's a very serious crime. We could all be sent to prison,' Rowan explained.

Jeremiah was inclined to dismiss their fears.

'No-one will know. Even if they see a deer has been killed, they'd never suspect us!'

Rowan could not believe what he was hearing.

'Of course they'll know. You did it in broad daylight. Half the county will know by now.'

'Oh Shh …' Jeremiah saw Bronwyn's eyes widen and decided to change track. '… eeesh! I guess I screwed up big time, huh?'

'Yes, big time.' Rowan was suddenly all business. 'But we mustn't dwell on that now. We've got to hide it.'

'That's the spirit. You hide it and I'll head him off at the pass. See if I can fool him by laying a false trail.' Jeremiah turned to go then checked himself.

'By the way, what does this gamekeeper look like?'

'Oh he's …' Rowan spread his arms wide, miming an enormous man.

'And he's got an enormous …' Bronwyn stroked imaginary hairs beneath her chin.

'Got ya!' Jeremiah hurried out.

7.

The large, bearded man walked slowly down the path that led through the woods. He was aided in his walking by a long pole that he had in his hands. From time to time he stopped to inspect the ground. Without a doubt there had been a killing here. The trail of blood was evidence of that. But this was the work of an expert. He had seen the contrivance of ropes and knew what that meant. Now it was just a matter of tracking him. The blood was still fairly fresh and headed in the direction of the farmhouse where that silly poet lived with his fair and, it had to be noted, buxom, wife. But he couldn't see either of them doing this. This was not the work of a poet. However, they had guests. That was well known. People from less civilized places. People who might very well think it perfectly all right to kill a deer just for the fun of it. It was his guess that a deer barbecue was even now being planned at the Rowan Jones farmhouse. This was a delicate matter and it might be best to take it up with the master himself, Lord Haverford.

He had been so deep in his thoughts that he had not noticed the man standing on the plank that crossed the narrow stream ahead. It's true the man was standing with an uncommon stillness and his clothing naturally blended in with the surrounding bushes and trees.

'Who are you sir?' he roared. 'You are trespassing on the demesne of Lord Haverford.' He wanted to make his authority clear from the start.

'I, sir,' Jeremiah said with a clear and defiant tone, 'am the descendent of Robin of Loxley. You have heard of him I dare say.'

'Robin of Loxley?' The Gamekeeper was bemused. 'What tomfoolery is this?'

'Robin Hood to you. And who might you be, oh great lumbering oaf? Are you a minion of the Sheriff of Nottingham?'

'Impertinent pup! Listen to me clearly! I am John Johnson. Head gamekeeper of this demesne and ...' As he spoke he moved closer to Jeremiah, planning to give him a good thumping.

'Do they call you Little John?'

'Ay! That's what some call me,' he gave a grimace of humour. 'But not more than once!'

Suddenly, and with surprising speed he whirled his long wooden pole and brought it down on the spot where Jeremiah had been standing. But Jeremiah had seen it coming from a long way off and had stepped back. Reaching behind a tree trunk he brought out his own wooden pole and the two of them began to fight. Up and down the plank over the stream they fought. First the gamekeeper had the advantage, then Jeremiah. The gamekeeper managed to land a heavy blow that nearly knocked Jeremiah into the stream but he managed to recover and go on to rain a number of telling blows on the gamekeeper who was forced to step back a few paces. Then once again the gamekeeper came back and with one hefty blow knocked Jeremiah clean off the bridge and into the sludgy bed of the stream.

'Hey!' Jeremiah shouted. 'That wasn't in the script.'

Suddenly there was the sound of a hunting horn. Coming out of the woods were a number of mounted men dressed in the armour and accoutrements of medieval knights. Again came the haunting sound of the horn as the horsemen reined in their mounts. The leading knight raised his visor. The Gamekeeper stepped back to address him.

'My Lord !' he bowed. 'One of the deer has been killed and it is my strong suspicion that this here whipper-snapper is the culprit.'

The knight drew his broadsword.

'By God! I'll have your intestines for garters!'

Jeremiah saw he was not in a good position to fight and started to wade through the oozing mud to the far side of the stream. The heavy silence that attended the scene as they tried to work out what was going to happen next was broken by the clatter of horse hooves as Ivan came on the scene with Barnaby behind him, clutching on for dear life. Unable to hold his position any longer he slid awkwardly to the ground. Quickly recovering his footing he unsheathed his own sword and held it out in front of him.

'On guard sir!' he glared as ferociously as he could. 'On my honour sir, I do challenge you. Or are you a coward?'

Lord Haverford wheeled towards him.

'My God, sir. You will feel the steel of my blade.'

He dismounted and strode towards Barnaby. The swords clicked together and the fight was on. But not for long. Soon Lord Haverford's sword was spinning uselessly into the air. Lord Haverford stopped in amazement.

'How extraordinary!'

'How so?'

'I have been told I am the second best swordsman in England. I can tell you this has never happened to me before.'

'And who, pray, is the best?'

'Oh someone you won't have heard of. Some flipperty-gibbet, some nouveau riche upstart by the name of St John Smythe. That's what they tell me.'

'Barnaby St John Smythe?' asked Barnaby.

'That's the man.' Lord Haverford nodded. 'So you've heard of him too.'

'I see him almost every day.'

'That so? Well, you can give him my regards. It seems I am now at best the third best swordsman in Britain.'

'You are still the second best. Allow me to introduce myself. Barnaby St John Smythe at your service.'

'Oh I say!' He struggled to extract his hand from his gauntlet. 'My honour indeed.' They shook hands. 'Forget what I said just now about ...'

Barnaby waved his hand airily.

'Consider it forgotten.'

'Delighted to make your acquaintance at last.'

'Perhaps you would care to join us for a spot of supper. I'd like you to meet a few people. I think you'll find them interesting. I believe we're planning a party.'

'Well, I'd be delighted.'

'Yes,' Jeremiah managed to break in. 'We're going to have the very best venison this side of the Atlantic.'

'Venison?' Lord Haverford's eyes glittered in pleasurable expectation 'Oh I say! I do like a spot of ...' His voice trailed off as he looked at the gamekeeper's stern expression. 'Venison you say?'

8.

The party was in full swing. Ayesha had finally cast off her reserve and was dancing a Berber dance to great applause. (Is she not a queen of the desert, thought Leona and clapped louder than anyone. Ayesha rewarded her with a quick smile.) Around and around she twirled flaunting her skirts at the men before whirling away. When she finished, Ivan took the floor and did a Cossack dance with much kicking and dancing from the haunches. Kono tried his hand at it and promptly fell over, to much laughter. Then Karl, on his strange, ostrich-like, prosthetic legs walked across the floor to Jade and bowing invited her to dance a tango with him. It was evident that he was a master at the highly charged, highly dramatic dance. It was equally evident that Jade had no understanding at all of what was required of her. She eventually realized that she was expected to mirror his moves, which she attempted to do, but with little success. Nevertheless, Karl kept her at it, to everyone's amusement. (And all the time, Leona watched Ayesha, saw her pain—why had Karl not asked her to dance? Ah, my sweet, Leona thought, taste the bitter berries of love. I can give you sweeter fruit. But Ayesha never once turned her eyes to Leona, never once gave her the chance to express her feelings.)

Then Solomon took out his violin and serenaded them

all with a plaintive Yiddish folk song which merged into a wedding dance which in turn became something recognizably by Bach. This in turn became a wild wailing of bluegrass. Musical form followed musical form seamlessly. When, at last he lowered the bow and bowed, the applause was deafening. Mad Mike took it upon himself at this moment to demonstrate a haka—that famous Pacific Island war dance—and with much grunting, tongue protrusion and facial grimacing he managed to scare the wits out of Ayesha and Jade who both recoiled with high pitched shrieks as he approached them. Yoshi and Toshi took courage from this display and since they couldn't do anything together without competing they went into a cacophony of chanting and waving hands at each other, throwing different numbers of fingers in the air. It was an old drinking game in which the winner was the one who guessed correctly the combined totals of the two hands. But since they both knew what the other was going to do they both won all the time. This curious display left the others in a state of polite bemusement as they had no idea what was going on. Then it was Leonardo's turn to entertain with his Neapolitan love songs. At the end of which Marguerite went up to him and bestowed on his glowing cheek a loud smack of a kiss.

'Marguerite! It's your turn. What are you going to do to entertain us?' Ivan shouted and the rest echoed the invitation.

'Not me!' she waved them away, but they called out her name again and again so in the end, with a stern face, she looked them all in the eye.

'OK! You asked for it. I will give you Baudelaire, Les Fleurs du Mal in the original. And you must listen:

Au Lecteur
La sottise, l'erreur, le péché, la lésine,
Occupent nos esprits et travaillent nos corps,

Et nous alimentons nos aimables remords,
Comme les mendiants nourrissent leur vermine.

They were all so bemused by this, delivered with all due seriousness, that they let her give her yet another verse:

Nos péchés sont têtus, nos repentirs sont lâches ;
Nous nous faisons payer grassement nos aveux,
Et nous rentrons gaiement dans le chemin bourbeux,
Croyant par de vils pleurs laver toutes nos taches.

'Ayeeah!!! What are you saying to us?' Jade called out.

'I am giving you culture!' Marguerite shouted back.

'Well, I think we've had enough of that high flown culture,' Jeremiah spoke languidly as he took to the stage with his banjo and began picking the strings. In no time at all everyone in the room was on their feet dancing and slapping their sides to the beat of the bluegrass music he played.

వ

After a while the music and dancing gave way to conversation, both genial and jovial. Jeremiah entertained the gamekeeper with tales of how he removed a skunk's stink glands and sent them to the local representative of the Ku Klux Klan. The gamekeeper, in turn, explained how he had used a weasel to terrify a local thug by dropping it into the thug's shirt and then gripping him tightly by the collar telling him, at the same time, that the weasel would eat his way into the man's … er … stomach, he said but meant something else. Lord Haverford was talking to Kono and Karl about the problems they had faced.

Bronwyn had cornered Rowan and was whispering urgently into his ear.

'Now. You must talk to him now. Lord Haverford can help you.'

'Are you sure? Maybe we should …?' Rowan dithered until Bronwyn folded her arms and glared at him.

'Now!'

A glare from Bronwyn was enough to set him on his way. But what should he say? How should he put it? But before he could launch himself into his speech, the door opened and in came Tom Jones followed by the Welsh national basketball team posing as his backing chorus. His voice drowned out even Jeremiah's banjo.

'It's not unusual to be loved by anyone
It's not unusual to have fun with anyone
but when I see you hanging about with anyone
It's not unusual to see me cry,
oh I wanna' die.'

This was greeted with loud applause. Bronwyn handed him a glass of beer which he raised to acknowledge the cheers and then put to his lips.

'No, seriously, now,' he looked around to see who he should be addressing and was pointed towards Rowan.' I heard what you were doing, and I thought to myself, that's something I'd like to support. So, how can I help?'

For the first time that evening there was a silence so complete you could have heard a snail fart. This was the question. This was the reason they were all there. But what exactly were they going to do? What? When? And where? The why? had already been taken care of and the who? was self-explanatory.

The answer came in an unexpected way. There was a timid knock on the front door and then (because someone hadn't closed it properly behind them!) it swung open revealing a person whose gender was not entirely clear. Dressed and made up like a woman, the face was nevertheless one that seemed more appropriate on a male body. It was, of course, Anna.

'Please come in and make yourself at home,' Bronwyn said with all due courtesy.

Anna smiled uncertainly. It had been a tough journey and now she had arrived. She wanted to savour this moment. At last, assured that she was indeed welcome she stepped in followed by four porters each carrying two heavy suitcases, which they deposited and then brought in two more each.

'I've just come from Paris,' Anna said, as if this explained everything.

'Now that is unusual,' Tom Jones murmured as he watched her pay off the porters and wave them away.

'Now!' she looked around at the assembled athletes. 'I have come to meet the great Welsh poet Mistair Rowan Jones.' Anna looked expectantly from one face to another (such strong and impressive faces, she thought).

'Ahem! That would be me, I expect, though I don't know that 'great' is really ...'

Her face did its best to hide the disappointment she felt.

'Mistair Jones. I am Anna. Anna Popelova. I used to be Dmitry Popelov until they forced me to take the drugs and ...' she swept her hand like a scythe across her groin. 'Now, as you can see ...'

'Come in,' Bronwyn insisted. 'Anna, please. Sit here. Have a drink. Some food.'

'Yes, please. That would be good. I have come such a long way and I am hungry.'

She allowed herself to be guided to a soft chair. A drink was placed in her hand. The hand went in the general

147

direction of her mouth and the drink disappeared.

'Ah, yes! That was good! I needed it! And now some …' she was holding out her hand for the plate of food that Bronwyn was bringing to her when she suddenly slapped herself on the forehead and jumped to her feet.

'What am I thinking? What am I doing? I must tell you about the bomb!'

'The bomb???!!!' Everybody cried out in alarm.

So Anna told them what she knew—and of course this entailed much back tracking (and side-ways tracking too). Somehow, during the telling of the story, Anna had managed to arrange it so that she was seated next to that august but oh so handsome aristocratic gentleman, Lord Haverford.

'Call me Bertie,' he had murmured in her ear.

She had a soft spot for aristocrats and it seemed he too might have felt a touch of electricity between them for he had let his hand rest lightly on her knee.

'So,' she concluded her story. 'President Osmanakhian the Terrible plans to explode a bomb at the London Olympic Games.'

'Oh no!' they all cried.

'Oh yes!' she insisted.

'You are so brave,' murmured Lord Haverford. 'And lovely too I may add.'

'How kind you are,' Anna replied and fluttered her eye lids.

There was a long silence then as they all chewed on this most indigestible news.

'We must do something,' Ayesha cried out. 'But what can we do?'

Leona took the opportunity to lean forward and put her arm around her shoulder.

'Surely we can do something,' she murmured and

Ayesha taking courage from these words nodded and gripped her hand with some force.

'Yes! We must do something to stop this madness.'

Leona was aware of nothing else but the warmth and feel of the hand that gripped hers. If only this moment could last forever.

'President Osman Osmanakhian of Transcaucasia?' Lord Haverford was suddenly thoughtful. 'Now that you mention it, the name seems familiar. I do believe he's staying with my good friend Freddy Fruhmanhoff. In fact, I've been invited there next Saturday, to a garden party in his honour.'

He beamed round the room.

'Isn't that a coincidence?'

Anna threw her arms round his neck and gave him a big wet kiss full on his mouth causing his eyebrows to pop up.

'Oh, well, I say!' Lord Haverford gasped as he emerged from Anna's embraces. He seemed flustered but not entirely disapproving.

'Now, maybe there is hope!' she declared. 'We must come up with a plan.'

Part Four

1.

F air summer was even now laying its hands across the green fields of England, now ablaze with a benevolent and humming indolence. Flowers ripened to the morning sun, opening their petals like fruit to be plucked. The air was filled with the warm fragrances of reds and pinks and oranges. The world was alive with the buzzing of insects as bees bounced from blossom to blossom. On days like this when even the greens of hedge and lawn, of leaf and weed shimmered and vibrated in the warm air, then to be in England was very Heaven.

And here, at this point, where a wide river lazily snaked through the flat, partly-wooded countryside, it was the very centre of Heaven. The Jacobean house was neither large, nor small. Size depends on the frame of reference. For Freddy Fruhmanhoff, of the New York Fruhmanhoffs, this was a modest, eight-bedroom house with several acres of garden that had been divided and sub-divided into a number of aesthetically distinct areas. These gardens—he liked to use the plural—included a maze where every year at least one child disappeared for as long as half an hour of sheer, shrieking terror, a terror that would mark the psyche of that child for the duration of their childhood, and sometimes beyond. Freddy always takes great care on these occasions to ooze sympathetic charm and to reinforce the psychic damage through subtle means. For example, he makes a point of giving the child a present. Not just any present, mind you, but an enormous life changing present—a jewel, perhaps, if it is a girl; a train set or a model aeroplane that really works if it's a boy. A present so stupendous that it will remain at one and the same time treasured and feared. It will be a permanent reminder of the dark forces that the child summoned to consciousness on that day when he or she was all alone in a dark, dark maze and there was no way to escape, no way at all. Certainly not before the dark spirits had ... (Hmmmmmm! Delicious just to think on it). It is always at this point, the point where the dark forces begin to incarnate, to take on meaty physical shape, that the child's mind shuts down. The black descends like a curtain. The mind knows that what it is trying to bring to awareness is so unspeakably (Unthinkably! Unimaginably!) awful. It is so awful that it simply cannot be comprehended.

Sadly, Freddy, though he appears a loving soul, gracious and warm, a constantly laughing and generous host, harbours dark secrets. He too was once caught in the coils of a maze when he was very, very young. He too screamed in panic and ran from the monstrous creations of his own mind. He too was given a teddy bear so darling and huggable that he took it everywhere with him, and although he thought he had forgotten the connection there were nights when he woke at three in the morning and saw across the room the marble eyes of the bear glitter in the pale moonlight that streaked across the room from the gap in the curtains that he insisted on or he would throw a tantrum, and glitter they did with evil intent.

And, many years later, it was in another maze, he was seduced by an older, very much older, female cousin of his sister's new husband. We should all, perhaps, be grateful that knowledge is thus passed down from one generation to the next. But Freddy did not feel this gratitude. Instead he found it an experience so mucky and tacky and yecchy—his own preferred vocabulary—that he has remained to this day a single man untouched by gossip. From time to time. there are rumours that he is to be outed. But nothing has ever come of any such attempts because no-one can be found with the first hand knowledge to make the claim credible.

I could go on and on about the maze. Strangely, however, more than the maze, it is the lawn that Freddy finds disturbing. He wonders if that is because he is one of the New York Fruhmanhoffs and not one of his Munich cousins or his Parisian affines. The European branches of his family are far more noted for muscular and adventurous outdoor activities—derring-do on the Cresta Run and so on. But he has never done very much in that line, or indeed in any other. Rich men of independent means, whose money is managed for them, need not do very much. Freddy does the minimum possible. But he likes to be affable. He enjoys parties. He enjoys having bizarre and outlandish guests to stay. He has the staff to deal with all the arrangements. All he has to do is don his mauve and yellow blazer and his straw boater and sally forth into the mingling throng wherever that mingling throng might be, around the breakfast table or on the lawn or even down by the river. But although he absolutely loves lawn parties the lawn itself sends an ever so slightly sinister shiver down his back. There is a definite touch of the macabre. As if some diaphanous dance of once-living sprites continues for ever after on the green lawns of Limbo, which just so happen to stretch from the kitchen of his house down to the river. Or is it Purgatory? There is a difference, he knows, but what the difference is he knows not. There is a life of the dead that continues alongside the life of the living but in a parallel dimension—but only a few have the gift of piercing the cosmic veil. He believes this because a nanny, Auntie Evelyn— (Auntie Evil! He would whisper to himself after she had left him alone in the darkness of his bedroom at night)—once told him so. He can still remember her vividly. For some reason he remembers the letters that came for her addressed to Miss Evelyn L Horne. He always tried to say this name as quickly as possible. He shook his head amused with himself and the sillinesses of youth. As for his unease with lawns, he has had counselling in the hope that educated probing will release him from the grip of the repressed traumatic memory that is presumed to be the cause, but no repressed traumatic memory can be found. He has forced both his parents to undergo counselling, too, to see if they can shed light on this odd tingle of aversion. To no avail. Lawns played no part that either could remember in their lives. Their fifty-room apartment did not have, as far as they could remember, any room with a lawn. What can it be, this nameless, faceless cause of his disaffection with lawns? Is it the threat of games implicit in a large lawn—bowls, badminton or tennis? Croquet? It seems not. Is it the implicit domestication of the field, making a carpet out of a prairie? Nope.

So, there it is! The lawn continues to smirk at him the fearful understated grimace of the dark unknown. There is nothing he can do about it. So, though he absolutely adores lawn parties, he has anxieties, no more than that (let us not exaggerate!), about the lawns that they are held on.

And on this day, the day of his annual garden party, he has managed to set aside this queasiness to supervise the arrangements. This is the only way he can feel connected. If he didn't supervise then there would be no need for him at all. So, to escape this sense of cosmic pointlessness, he shouts and waves his arms and demands shifts and changes. Then he countermands these earlier instructions when he eventually realizes what everyone else has realized long ago. And so it is that the long tables are set up. The marquee is raised. The guy ropes are hammered into the earth with mallets. The tables are covered with immaculate white table cloths. Plates and silverware are laid out. The food itself is on its way he is assured when he starts fussing again. Then he steps back and he sees that his interventions are not just useless but exacerbating the difficulties. Perhaps, he muses, this is how God feels. God wanted to get stuck in but he found that he was just making a mess of things. So he too took a step back and let it just happen. Freddy rather liked the metaphor (or was it a simile?) of God. It made him feel important. It gave a grand perspective to his uselessness. And the lawn stretched away into the distance. Sometimes he can hear the cry of the lawn beckoning him, saying: 'Come. Follow me. Come to the end of the lawn.' And he is tempted. Believe me, he is tempted. One day he will follow that call and it will take him to … where exactly? If only he knew where the lawn wanted him to go. Of course, the prosaic answer might be that the lawn wants him to go and drown himself in the river. Why drown? Why not just swim? Or boat? Or raft, like Huckleberry Finn? (Come now, you're being silly — Ed.)

But, today of all days, Freddy cannot sink into any lawn-centred reverie. He has guests. It was his banking cousin, Baron Karl-Heinz von Fruhmanhoff, of the München Fruhmanhoffs who had invited President Osman Osmanakhian to be Freddy's guest during the Olympic Games. Karl-Heinz was still very much involved in the family businesses that laid the foundation for their stupendous wealth—minerals, salt and so on—in the early seventeenth century. Transcaucasia—with its ruby mines, the finest outside Burma it is said, and its great salt deposits—was a tantalizing prospect. Contracts were, even now, being negotiated that would lay the foundation of their wealth's continuance for yet another generation or two. So keeping President Osman Osmanakhian sweet was very much at the top of Freddy's priorities.

He turned from the preparations outside to see how things were getting on indoors.

2.

Eight bedrooms are not enough for a presidential party but Osman Osmanakhian has managed to squeeze himself and his closest associates into the accommodation provided. Freddy has, of course, had to relinquish his master bedroom to his guest. He has moved himself to what was once a porter's lodge by the main gate. This is a cold, damp, and altogether grim building but Freddy is a solid citizen and takes the long view. He will put up with no end of discomfort as long as it benefits the Fruhmanhoff enterprise. 'Freddy's a good man!' he imagines the others saying when his name comes up. 'Always ready to rally round!' The truth is, Freddy has an enormous need to be useful. He understands that the stagnant, turgid pool of wealth that has accumulated over generations and which is now very much in his lap, his custody, his guardianship, is not his. It belongs to the enterprise as a whole. It belongs to Fruhmanhoffs not yet born. He trusts that they too will tend this wealth as he has tended it, assiduously and without greed. Better two pounds tomorrow than one pound today, his father always told him and Freddy agrees. But while he has the use of it, he is happy to put his snout in the trough and snuffle at the goodies that this wealth provides him with. He is happy to be the accidental beneficiary of the largesse inherited from financially sober and strategically adept ancestors. He does thank them, when he remembers to, as he passes their portraits on the walls of the entrance. Life is good. It could of course be better. But when he has this thought he tries to set it aside firmly. Life is good enough, he thinks. Let that be the end of the matter.

But good enough as his life is, there are certain discomforts that playing host to Osman Osmanakhian has imposed on him. There is, first and foremost, the question of the presidential well-being. It is assumed there are persons who nurture the intention of negatively impacting that well-being. Freddy is therefore subject to the petty and vexatious security measures that accompany any head of state. So whenever Freddy has the desire to launch himself upstairs—it is one of his secret pleasures to take a short run and see how many of the lower stairs he can leap over (his record is five)—he is sharply deterred by the outstretched arm of a bald bodyguard (Freddy calls them the baldyguards). This blocking movement and the subtle twitch of the bodyguard's other hand towards some presumed weapon—a cosh? a firearm? An electric stun gun?—hidden beneath the fold of his dark coat is sufficient to cool Freddy's impetuousness.

Having initially intended to have a chin-wag (his words) with the Oz Man, as the president allowed himself to be called by his host, Freddy veered suddenly away from the staircase and headed for the kitchen. Here he found a bustling purposefulness that quite entranced him. He needed to be out of the way of things but he couldn't stand the thought of self-exile to his grim porter's lodge. He displaced a cat from a corner chair and sat down. It was his intention to have a brief rest, to absent himself from the preparations, for a short while, in order to prepare himself. The warmth of the room and his own cerebral vacancy soon lulled him into sleep.

&

Meanwhile, upstairs, President Osman Osmanakhian was going through his morning exercise routine with the Precious Presidential Ornament. She has choreographed this from various scenes taken from The Sound of Music. Together, it was as if they are Julie Andrews prancing across alpine meadows. This is one of President Osmanakhian's happiest moments of the day. Especially when they come to their own special tiptoeing version of 'Doe, a deer, a female deer; ray a touch of golden sun ...'

Oh, he was happy. He was on the brink of a spectacular success. If only he knew where Anna was. Somehow she had slipped away from his spies, along with four porters and sixteen pieces of luggage. You had to admire her. But she couldn't stay hidden forever. His men would catch up with her. And when they did ...! He felt an evil cackle rise in his throat. Oh yes! When they did find her, then ...! Then ...! But, there it was: the slightest of slight imperfections on the perfection of the day. He still had not settled on the perfect punishment. Then what? Boil her in vats of pig fat? Bah! That was too good for her. It would come to him, the perfectly apt reward for all this irritation she was causing him. Until then ...! She would fester in the dankest, darkest dungeon in the whole of Transcaucasia. He could see it now. She couldn't elude him forever.

'Just one more time, now!' the Precious Presidential

Ornament urged him on. 'On your tippy toes. Doe, a deer, a female deer ...' He followed her every move in an agony of delight, as she mimed her fingers playing a piano.

3.

The guests were starting to arrive. The essence of an English garden party is to choose a day of surprising warmth and then to make everyone sweat it out in the most inappropriate clothing. So it was that the mercury had risen and the ladies were emerging, clutching their hats, from air-conditioned chauffeur driven limousines. Freddy had been woken up and was now doing what few people do better. At hand shaking and hand kissing and the giving of gallant compliments and engaging in laughing man-to-man banter he was a master. 'Good old Freddy!' he imagined he could hear people thinking as he waved them through the house and out into the gardens beyond where the marquee stood and waiters and waitresses, dressed in black and white, were holding trays of drinks and snacks. A small orchestra went through the motions of tuning up and then, at a nod from the violinist, launched into an uplifting rendition of Basin Street Blues. The sound wafted pleasantly across the lawns.

Already groups of guests were strolling down the newly mown lanes towards the river embankment. 'Good old Freddy!' they said, meaning good old them for being on Freddy's guest list for there was no more delightful way to spend an afternoon than to stand around in rather stiff clothes showing off the line and shape of one's honed body—honing requires time and access to equipment and expertise which

requires money, so honed body equals sizeable income—
while people in boats slowly passed by and ogled them with
overt, and indeed blatant, jealousy. 'Good old Freddy!'

But not all the boat people were passing by. One boat, a
racing scull, suddenly veered towards the landing steps. The
rower was a well-dressed man in a rather flamboyant bright
yellow blazer. Shipping his oars, he let the boat glide quietly
the last few yards. Curious at this intrusion, a group stood and
stared at him. It was only now that they registered with some
shock that he had a striking tattoo across his dark, Polynesian
face. He stepped out of the scull with athletic ease and tied his
boat up to the dock. He then strode towards the nearest group,
a young Indian couple and a blonde woman.

'I reckon you're all friends of old Freddy? Am I right?'
He shook hands amiably all round.

There was a very visible relaxation. He was all right. A
bona fide guest. He knew Freddy. They nodded and smiled,
making room for him in their group. But Mad Mike had no
intention of being detained.

'I expect I'll find him up by the house.' He turned and
was about to leave when the blonde woman, no longer in the
first blush of youth, tucked her arm into his.

'How do you know Freddy?' she asked.

'Oh me and Freddy? We go way back.' Mad Mike
grinned wondering what yarn to spin. 'Freddy came through
Oz a while ago. I showed him around.' He didn't want to get
caught out on details and anyway sheilas liked to do the
talking.

'And what about yourself?'

Here she giggled and whispered in his ear.

'I'll tell you a little secret.'

'Go on then?'

'I'm an art assessor.'

159

'Oh yes?' Mad Mike wondered why she had changed the subject.

'I like a bit of art myself.'

She laughed as if he had made a deliberate joke.

'I value paintings and artworks for insurance purposes.'

'Is that right? I bet Freddy's got a masterpiece or two on his walls.'

Her eyes twinkled.

'Total value £35 million.'

Mad Mike whistled.

'And that's just this house. I haven't seen his New York pad but I'm told that ...'

By this time he had disengaged her from her original group of friends and she was walking slowly up the garden with him towards the house. She was good camouflage he decided and you never knew .... Her name was Marla, she said.

'Quick work!' said the young man admiringly to his female companion as he watched them drift away from the group.

'Who by?' she responded. They sniggered and turned again to look at the river.

'Whoah!' said the man, in sudden surprise. Standing about twenty feet away was perhaps the handsomest man either of them had ever seen. He was almost naked. In fact it took a sharp—and indeed prolonged—inspection on her part to determine that he wasn't. He had been smeared in a greeny-grey coating of paint and was standing completely still, a living statue. He was still wet, having clearly emerged from the river.

'Oh Freddy is such a joker!' the girl exclaimed and came close to inspect this hunk of a man. 'Delicious,' she thought. 'If only ...' and she looked once more to see if maybe he might be

160

naked, just a little. But he had been cleverly and discretely covered with leggings that held an imitation fig leaf in place. Just then their attention was distracted by the arrival of two more couples that they knew. Air kissing and cheek buffing accomplished, the Indian woman turned to show her friends this new visual treat. 'Come and look at ...' she said and turned to point to where the statue had been standing but he was no longer there.

'Oh!'

She was disappointed. She looked all round but couldn't see where he had gone. He was nowhere to be seen.

'He's gone.'

'Who's gone?'

She could only shake her head. She couldn't explain. Was it an image? Or a feeling? A promise or an intimation? She felt a stab of sadness. Like a dark wind blowing. A presentiment of death. Something of great beauty was suddenly no longer there. So life too passes. She shivered and turned back to her husband, letting her body rest against him. She took one of his hands in hers and caressed it with an affection that surprised him, that reminded him of those months when they were engaged some years ago. The others saw it too and were jealous.

❧

At more or less precisely the same time a pink Rolls drove up to the gate. Lord Haverford leaned out of the window and waved his invitation card at the security guard who inspected it.

'Lord and Lady Haverford?'

'That's us!'

The guard handed the ticket back and waved him in. The Rolls moved sedately up the drive to the parking area that other staff directed him towards. Perkins parked and then went and opened the rear door. Lord and 'Lady' Haverford emerged. With Anna on his arm Lord Haverford strolled towards the music and the marquee. Leaving the car door ajar, Perkins busied himself with buffing various car surfaces. As he did so, he looked around. No-one was paying any attention to him. When he was sure they were not being observed he rapped lightly on the bonnet. This was the signal they had been waiting for. One after the other all the athletes, including the members of the Welsh basketball team, emerged from the car. Some went and mingled with the guests while others were dressed as waiters and waitresses. The last to emerge was Rowan Jones himself, looking more than a little rumpled and disgruntled. He was one of those people who can never look smart, no matter what they do. He dusted himself down and then sauntered as best he could towards the lawns and in particular towards the champagne that he could see glinting, fizzily, a pale yellow, in the midday sun.

When they had all gone, Perkins discreetly closed the door and set himself to wait. He had with him a volume of Proust to while away the time.

Jeremiah had instinctively aimed for the back door followed, not so instinctively, perhaps, but after some existential cogitation, by Marguerite. Just inside the door there was a pantry area where two waiters were having a cigarette. Jeremiah put his finger to his lips to caution her to be quiet. She nodded and waited.

'They treat you as if you weren't there!' one of the waiters was complaining.

'You're invisible,' the other agreed. 'People don't see waiters.'

'Pisses me off!'

'Don't let it get to you. It's normal. Just the way things are. You'll get used to it.'

Marguerite peeked into the room and saw there were two trays of snacks waiting to be taken out. She nudged Jeremiah and pointed at them. He nodded. They crept in, picked them up and went out again. The waiter who had been complaining took one last puff on his cigarette before dropping it to the ground and stubbing it out. He turned to pick up a tray.

'Hey!'

'What's the matter?'

'Where have the trays gone?'

'Yeah!' the other looked around in surprise. 'We left them just there.'

They looked at each other dumbfounded and shook their heads.

'Old houses like this give me the creeps.'

'You think it was ghosts?'

'Well …?'

He left the thought dangling.

'Now what do we do?'

❧

Jeremiah and Marguerite were by now making their way through the house offering their snacks to the few people they passed — mostly security people of one sort or another. As they approached the main staircase, there was a sudden commotion. President Osmanakhian and his First Lady were descending. The path before them was being cleared by security persons talking into ear-pieces. Jeremiah and Marguerite made to offer them snacks but were waved aside. As they watched the presidential party make its leisurely progress towards the glass doors, Jeremiah noticed that the number of guards at the foot of the steps had been reduced to one but he decided to get an over-view of the house and gardens before making any move in that direction. The problem was that no-one knew what they were looking for. The plan was to spread throughout the house and gardens to see if anyone could find anything at all that might give a hint of plans to plant a bomb.

In the garden, a diminutive Chinese girl was going through a variety of juggling and acrobatic routines. Freddy couldn't recall that they'd ordered entertainments but she was jolly good whoever she was. He made a mental note to book her again. But he didn't have time to watch her. He had work to do. Glad handing. And here was the Oz Man himself.

'At last!' he smiled in greeting. 'Welcome to the festivities.'

President Osmanakhian allowed his flaccid hand to be shaken. Their host was proving to be a somewhat tiresome man.

'And I kiss your hand,' Freddy said in his best Hungarian manner (for some reason he assumed that Hungary and Transcaucasia were similar in culture), bowing to the First Lady and placing his lips on her glove. Up until now everything that happened did so in harmony with expectations. But there was, on the back of the glove being kissed, a delicate Transcaucasian oil whose scent seemed to shoot straight up Freddy's nostrils to the pleasure centre of his brain.

The First Lady's eyes twinkled with wicked pleasure. Pampelweed oil was known to have any number of effects. Unlike other drugs which imposed their pharmacology on the psyche, pampelweed had the reverse effect of lying back and encouraging the psychic undertones to emerge, to feel at ease, to start undressing so as to reveal themselves fully. For the First Lady this resulted in an exaggerated sensuality. Unfortunately, she believed that this was its effect on everyone. For the President it had the impact of releasing his demons, the voices in his head, the personas in his psyche. And Freddy? Well, Freddy's head span for a moment before he recovered himself. He let go of the Precious Presidential Ornament's hand and looked round dizzily for something to say. Perhaps he was looking for the Chinese acrobat but instead his eyes alighted on the group standing nearby. There, fortuitously, was Lord Coe talking to Lord Haverford and his … dear God! Who was that woman? Freddy was appalled. Aesthetic issues were first and foremost in his world. And that woman did not belong to any aesthetic scheme of things that he had ever come across. But Haverford couldn't keep his hands off her. The silly old buffer. Freddy might have reconsidered his act, but the shot of Transcaucasian pampelweed had slowed him down. He was already committed.

'Ah! Yes! Allow me to introduce you to …'

Before he could finish his sentence the bloody baldyguards were busy frisking them, patting everyone down the sides and up the legs. Everyone, of course, except Lord Coe who had that athlete's knack of seeing the gap, seeing the move five yards before it was made, and who had simply stepped back and watched the proceedings with a slightly disdainful look. Lord Haverford however was not exempt. He twitched and squirmed.

'Oh I say! Is this necessary? I'm very ticklish you know.'

When the guards were sure there were no would-be assassins amongst them they stepped back and formed a huddle behind the president. From this location they practiced their scan-the-crowd and scan-the-roof and scan-the-horizon skills all the while speaking in an incomprehensible murmur into microphones. Who were they talking to? What were they saying? Freddy's encounter with pampelweed was not yet over. Something was shooting streaks of purple everywhere he looked. And was that greeny-grey, almost naked man standing not twenty yards away a figment of his imagination or not? Something was definitely playing with his perceptions. And the lawn was beckoning to him again.

'Come, Freddy,' the voice whispered. 'Come to the end of the lawn.'

Who said that? He whirled round. But there was no-one behind him. Unless you counted those two Japanese men who were doing violent hand signals at each other. Their mouths were moving but no sound seemed to be emerging. Strange, he thought suddenly, how everyone says that all Japanese look the same. He laughed. Ridiculous! Why, you just had to look at their ...! Freddy's brow furrowed with the effort of concentration. Or their .... He tried to focus on a different feature. But whatever he looked at—nose, chin, mouth, the way they stood, the way they moved—he could not see the differences he knew to be there. They were as different as chalk and ... er ... chalk. Come to think of it, they did look remarkably similar. What had happened to him? This wasn't like him at all. Turning back he noticed that a number of the younger ladies had clustered round the living statue and were giggling. Even the Presidential Ornament had gone to inspect him. Who had organized these entertainments? He didn't remember being consulted on this at all. Was he being omitted from the must-be-informed list? Was he that useless? Of course now wasn't the time to go into this but first thing tomorrow he would call a meeting. It just wasn't on! Unless of course it was a surprise present to him from the Oz Man! Now that he thought of it, this was much more likely. In that case it was a delight and he would tell him so at the first opportunity.

'A wonderful ...!' he gestured about him with a smile, expecting his listener to finish the sentence for him with a nod. But his listener showed no interest in the proceedings whatsoever.

President Osmanakhian had been studying events with increasing nervousness. Not only was this house with its pathetic imitations of bedrooms hideously small but out here in the garden there were people all around. And they were ignoring him. This was intolerable. How was it being allowed? And then there was this woman, this caricature of Anna, being flaunted at him. Every time he looked at her, she fluttered her saucy eyes at him. Outrageous. And in front of the Precious Ornament herself. No wonder she had gone walking. Oh Anna! Where are you?

Lord Coe had sensed he was about to be eclipsed in the attention-garnering business and had, smiling, faded even further into the background and was just getting ready to move on when he encountered a very short, determinedly jovial man.

'Sticky, what?'

'Ah yes!' Lord Coe responded. 'Indeed it is.'

The man held out his hand.

'Barnaby St John Smythe at your service.'

Lord Coe acquiesced in the matter of having his hand shaken. The name was familiar. Or was it? In what context?

'Ah yes,' he smiled using gambit number three. 'You're in … um?'

Barnaby countered this strategy by raising his eyebrows enquiringly, interested to know in what context he might have come to Lord Coe's attention.

'I'm sorry,' the great man said at last after a silence that was growing increasingly embarrassing. 'You'll have to remind me.'

'Foil perhaps?' Barnaby said and twirled his hand.

'Foil?' Lord Coe did not grasp the allusion immediately. Was it catering then? 'Aluminium?'

Barnaby laughed and made a more explicit gesture of fencing.

167

'Oh yes, quite. Silly me. In the team?'

Barnaby gave an equivocal gesture. Lord Coe gave himself a mental smack on the forehead—of course! The man was so short he was probably in the Paralympics.

'Oh well, better luck next time perhaps.'

Barnaby grinned politely and decided it was time to change the subject.

'So tomorrow the Olympic Flame will be lit.'

Lord Coe nodded and smiled. It would be his proudest moment. Eight long years it will have been. And he will have brought the games home—and done it in style. Yes. He could be properly proud.

'How are the security arrangements?' Barnaby enquired. 'I heard there was a bomb threat.'

'Bomb threat?' Lord Coe hadn't heard of one. 'I don't think …'

'Yes. Definitely a bomb threat,' he persisted. He wanted to assess their level of preparedness, perhaps even hint at beefing up measures.

Lord Coe was feeling increasingly unsure of his ground. It was time to fall back on gambit nine.

'I couldn't possible comment.' And tapped his nose to suggest greater knowledge than he in fact possessed. He'd have to get on to his security team right away to find out the details. This Smythe person seemed to be quite definite. In the distance he could see a file of short men followed by a rather tall black man entering the maze at speed. It seemed they were being pursued by a security guard. Or maybe the guard was just lending a helping hand. It was difficult to tell at this distance. His instincts kicked in and he decided that it was probably time to go. He had made an appearance and he was, as everyone knew, an extremely busy man, so … where was the host?

Throughout the garden, guests huddled in puddles of connectedness. To be alone, to be unconnected to any huddle, was a fate beyond humiliation. Stay together! This was the great unstated imperative. For girls especially. Men were expected from time to time to prowl like beasts in the jungle, looking for mates. But a girl would be ill-advised to desert her huddle. But if this imperative were to be allowed to persist it would make for a very stodgy afternoon. For this reason acts like Jade's juggling and acrobatics, or Leonardo's majestic immobility were so useful. Individuals forgot the great imperative and allowed themselves to be seduced away from their groups. Entranced for a while by the delights of the spectacle, a person would suddenly come to his or her senses and feel that rush of fear, the fear of solitude, the fear of desertion. Marla had been there and was wise to her soul. As she dragged this new exciting man along, she saw the competition of girls ogling Leonardo and clutched more tightly to her own man. Though he was a hunk, she thought with a touch of regret as she passed him by. Another time perhaps.

'Let me show you some of Freddy's etchings,' she murmured in Mad Mike's ear and guided him towards the house. Since this was his destination too, he was happy to be dragged along. It seemed she was known to the staff so there was no impediment to their progress.

'This is the Matisse,' she pointed to a drawing that could have been a Matisse or a Michelangelo for all he knew, or indeed cared. 'Look at that line. Look at those shapes. Aren't they just darling?'

There was no question about it, 'darling' was the mot juste, or as Mad Mike expressed it: 'Couldn't have put it better myself.'

'And here ...' she dragged him down the corridor to a

small alcove, 'is the Botero.'

'Fat bastard, ain't he!'

Marla could tell he was only joking and gave him a playful poke in the ribs.

'Hey!'

'Now, I'm going to show you the Gauguin, which is definitely the best painting in the whole collection. You'll like the Gauguin.'

'I will?'

'It'll remind you of home, I expect'

'It will?'

She dragged him to the hallway where the staircase ascended to the first floor. She smiled at the guard and mouthed 'The Gauguin' at him. As if he knew what she was talking about!

'You are going to love what I am going to show you,' she said with a naughty look. 'You're in for a surprise.'

So are you, he thought to himself as they slowly climbed the stairs, looking at the portraits of Fruhmanhoffs past.

'Horrible lot,' she whispered. 'Freddy's the only decent human in the whole family. They say they were burghers but I tell you they were right buggers too. The whole lot of them give me the creeps. I keep telling Freddy to get Hockney to paint his portrait but he knows the rest of the family will disapprove. Too unserious if you know what I'm saying.'

Mad Mike had long ago stopped understanding a word of what she was saying. He was looking around for anything that looked as if it might be a bomb.

'The Gauguin's in here,' she said finally, pulling him into one of the bedrooms.

❧

Out in the garden, most of the others were idly wondering

from group to group to see if they could overhear any conversation that might give a clue to what they were supposed to be looking for.

In one circle, a rather podgy man with a grey moustache and a definite stutter was telling a story.

'So bomb ...' Kono, who was passing by with an empty tray, pricked up his ears. '... bomb ... bombardier, I said to him, what is your view?' Kono relaxed and walked on. Ayesha too thought for a moment she might be on to something.

'The bomb ...' said one rather stout woman to her companion. Ayesha paused and looked at the sky as if assessing it for rain. '... the bombastic fool!' Ayesha turned and smiled at Leona who just happened to be standing behind her. She shook her head. No. this wasn't it.

It was Marguerite who, passing by another group—she was amused to see the elderly twins (those twins that we last met at Osmanakhian's Transcaucasian fortress) speaking in an intensely animated way to each other—heard the following snippet of conversation, almost hissed:

'What is the time?' asked one of the twins

'Ten past four,' the other answered.

They had looked then at each other with an intense excitement.

'So ...!'

'Exactly!'

'The bomb ...!'

'Will go off in exactly twenty four hours!'

And there was a sudden bout of handshaking and jumping up and down and laughter. She walked on pretending to have heard nothing but as soon as she could, she alerted Jeremiah that this was the group to keep an eye on. He in turn alerted Solomon who signalled to Ayesha. Just then the basketball team emerged from the maze no longer followed by any security guard and Ayesha whispered the information to the leader. The whisper got passed down the line.

❧

President Osmanakhian had not been able to take his eyes off Anna for some time now and she had retreated behind a fan which she now fluttered furiously. The Precious Ornament had returned to the President's side and he had gallantly kissed her hand. He was well aware of how charming these gallantries seemed to the stiff English and he wished above all to cut an exotic and, more importantly, a memorable figure. The scent of pampelweed released the tether on his psyche yet another notch. Finally he could stand it no longer.

'We have met before, I think,' he said addressing Anna directly.

Anna tittered and whispered something in Lord Haverford's ear. It was he who responded.

'She is sure she would remember if she had.'

A single cloud in the sky cast a sudden shadow over the group.

The Precious Ornament was a jealous and precise logician of the emotions.

'But the question is: does she remember?' she demanded and glared directly at her rival.

'I never forget a face,' the President persisted.

'Only faces?' Anna's fan was fluttering even more furiously.

'It was in Paris. We danced the whole night long.'

'The whole night? Dancing?' Anna sighed and shook her head. 'That wasn't me.'

'I remember it well. You wore blue and I wore grey.'

'You wore out.'

172

'You see! It was you. You do remember.'

'Not me. Someone else.'

'It was you!'

'Remember where you are.'

'Oh Anna! It is you!'

'I am Lady Haverford.' Her accent was strong and unmistakable.

Osmanakhian could take it no longer. The seething ferment of his emotions were too much for him to contain.

'Arrest this woman! Take her to the dungeons!'

Silence fell across the lawn as necks craned to see what was going on with that funny man the president of where-was-it?

'Doesn't he have such a wonderful sense of humour?' Anna said throatily and to Osmanakhian's mortification they all laughed. How could she do this to him? Him? Osmanakhian the Great! Osmanakhian the Liberator! Osmanakhian the Fantastic! He had at various times given himself all these titles and many more.

Freddy had been watching this exchange with mounting horror. Was it his perception or was Osmanakhian actually fragmenting? One minute he was a lion tamer, the next a ballerina. Then he was a giant monitor lizard, snaking its head here and there while its tongue flickered in and out. A molecular instability was at work. Or, alternatively, he thought, and much more logically, he, Freddy, was going mad. But if it was more reasonable to assume he was going mad, then surely, if he was mad, he wouldn't be attracted to the more reasonable explanation? Therefore he was not mad. But if he was not mad then the most reasonable explanation was that he was mad. This didn't make any sense at all. It was a paradox. Or a conundrum. One or the other. He was forever getting these words confused.

Solomon approached the group with an expression of becoming gravity on his face. On his tray were a dozen or so glasses of wine. He offered these to the cluster of security guards standing near the President's group. The guards looked round to make sure no-one was looking and feeling that the afternoon was going well and they could afford a little relaxation, each took a glass and quickly drained the contents. Recovering the empty glasses, Solomon moved on looking for his next target for the wine was spiked with a powerful incapacitating agent. Behind him he heard the tell-tale thump of a body hitting the ground, followed by two others. His line of retreat took him close to the Precious Ornament who caught sight of him and clicking her fingers imperatively, beckoned him to her. Before he could stop her she had taken one of the glasses. Barnaby, who had been supervising this part of the proceedings (Perkins had provided the drug), immediately saw what had happened and moved to head off the problem.

'Madam President. What an honour.'

'Oh hello!' she tittered when she had finally located him below her normal line of sight. 'How cute!'

'I assure you madam, I am not the slightest bit cute.'

'How sad then.'

'Not at all sad, I assure you. I find my height gives me a perspective on life that has its own rewards.'

The Precious Ornament bent down and Barnaby took the opportunity to relieve her of her drink. From this reduced altitude, she saw his point of view on the world, one that emphasized the curvaceous turn of a trim buttock. She turned back to Barnaby and gave him a wicked wink.

'You naughty boy!'

He shrugged.

'Now give me back my drink.'

'First I will show you a trick.'

'A magic trick? How I love magic!' she exclaimed.

Barnaby threw the contents of the glass over his shoulder without looking and the wine splashed into the face of a passing bodyguard who had come to see what had happened to his comatose colleagues. The contents caught him full in the face and he found himself licking it. A few seconds later, as he was inspecting his colleagues, he too quietly toppled over, falling on top of the pile of bodies, and lay perfectly still.

'That wasn't a very good trick,' she complained and before anyone could do anything to stop her, she had taken a second glass off the tray and knocked it back. Barnaby had started to lift his hands in apology. Now he stood in frozen horror as he waited for the inevitable.

'There!' she said. 'I have a very good head for wine.' She handed him the second glass as she gently toppled backwards into Solomon's arms. Solomon had somehow managed to pass his tray to Leonardo who happened to be beside him, surrounded by the inevitable cluster of giggling girls. He in turn passed it along. It was not for an Italian Olympian to carry trays of glasses at garden parties. Mr Berlusconi would not approve.

'I told you not to drink so much!' President Osmanakhian hissed at her but he was secretly relieved by this turn of events. It meant he could interrogate Anna—for surely he was not mistaken? This was Anna?—without her looking jealously on.

'Take her to her room!' he waved imperiously and turned his back on them.

It was with some surprise that Barnaby and Solomon found themselves in charge of the recumbent First Lady but Barnaby was quick to see the possibilities. He waved Jeremiah and Marguerite over and indicated to Leonardo that he would be more useful remaining a centre of attraction in the garden. Yoshi and Toshi joined the group and Barnaby instructed them to march ahead, clearing the way. Together they carried the First Lady to the house and up the stairs, the security guards along the way waving them through. Now where?

Something of this bubble of activity found its way into the kitchens where Ivan had found himself a cosy spot in the corner on top of the cat which he had sat on for the warmth of it. The cat had screeched and then fallen silent. If it was dead they could skin it and make some stew, he thought. Here was everything he wanted in life: warmth, food and fat people. Oh how he loved the wobble of fat. Fat arms, fat bottoms and that oh so delectable fatness of large bosoms. This was paradise. The smell of fat sizzling in a pan and the sight of mottled flesh flapping. Forget the Olympics! He would spend the rest of his days sucking at the blackened rotting stubs of his teeth as he savoured the textures of the food that his memory recalled.

But there was clearly something going on—he could hear banging and thought he heard Solomon's voice—and he owed it to his new friends (though how far could he trust them?) to be involved. Perhaps. It was normal for him to constantly assess and reassess every action and reaction. In the camps his life had depended on it. Who was to say the same didn't apply here? But his instincts told him his new friends were good people. He had learnt to trust these instincts. So, very reluctantly, and with an expression of infinite sadness—a sadness that welled up from the distant Steppes of his soul— he got up and walked out into the corridor. He was just in time to find Rowan, clutching a bottle of champagne, meandering rather drunkenly along. He took the bottle and had a swig. The bubbles promptly irrigated his nostrils. Ah yes! He'd forgotten this particular trick that champagne played.

'Where did they go?' Rowan asked, clearly worse for wear.

'Who?'

'Everybody. With that bloody man's wife.'

A group orgy with a Head of State's wife? He presumed it was that bloody man. This was not to be missed. And where did people have orgies? Bedrooms! He looked up. Rowan looked up. They looked at each other.

'Up the stairs maybe?'

So up the stairs they went.

❧

'Anna!' Osmanakhian wailed plaintively. 'Will you not change your mind?'

Again she twittered into Lord Haverford's ear. He then passed on the message.

'She says her mind and body are one. She will change one when she changes the other.'

The sky was now clear, a deep clear blue, from horizon to horizon, except for one minute dark grey piece of fluff that hovered, clearly deliberately, between the sun and Freddy Fruhmanhoff's lawn, casting a shadow on the three foot square occupied by President Osmanakhian.

'Anna, we need you.' His eyes beseeched her.

'Lady Haverford says,' Lord Haverford replied, having been fully briefed by the lady beside him, 'that she needs herself.'

'Anna, think of the glory!'

'Lady Haverford remembers when she had something that rose gloriously every morning. A glory that was firm and hard and gave meaning to each new day.'

'Anna, that can be rectified!'

'Lady Haverford wonders if you are entirely to be

trusted.'

'Trust?' Osmanakhian stepped back as if assaulted. 'Anna? You talk to me of trust? Who was it who ran off with the camel herder in Kashgent? With the Tirgiz pyramid guide in Sumarchand?'

Anna's fan shaking was now furious.

'Not to mention the canary breeder of Bakla-Takla!'

'Lady Haverford says that they took her as they found her.'

'But they took you!'

'And gave me back to myself.' Anna retorted, for the first time directly addressing herself to Osmanakhian.

'Arrest her!' He shouted again and a humorous tinkle of laughter slid from huddle to huddle. 'Such a good joke!' they thought. 'Such a funny man!'. Flustered at the lack of action, Osmanakhian turned to snap his fingers at whichever of his bodyguards was nearest. It was only then that he saw the piles of bodies and realised his security had been compromised.

'Back to the rooms!' he called out and turning his back on Anna he strode towards the doors to the house. Freddy watched in stunned bemusement as he saw the quivering of lizards' heads flicker forked tongues from the collar of Osmanakhian's presidential uniform. The madness was getting closer. He watched as the other members of the president's party hurried to catch up with Osmanakhian. The garden suddenly felt momentarily lonelier, then, just as suddenly, it felt lighter and happier. The musicians—ever sensitive to atmosphere and mood—stopped playing Summertime and launched into a version of Purple Haze. Someone told a nasty bit of gossip to much laughter. And in this way the moment passed. The party had teetered momentarily but now it was saved.

Meanwhile, upstairs, the clatter of feet on the steps

alerted everyone to the imminent arrival of the Osmanakhian party. Having deposited the First Lady on one of the beds—a bed that had seemed strangely lumpy until Mad Mike and Marla had rather sheepishly emerged on either side buttoning up what had been unbuttoned and buckling up what had been unbuckled—they had fanned out to all the rooms to search them for secret plans or code books or bottles of invisible ink or for anything that looked remotely like a bomb.

Only Karl remained outside on the landing holding his tray of drinks. Osmanakhian hurtled past him paying no notice.

'Check your rooms!' Osmanakhian shouted and Officer Pavlov and the two scientists headed towards the end room where Kono and Ayesha just had time to dive under the bed before the door opened. Leona, not quick enough to join them, simply stood still in a corner holding a tray of glasses—but since she was clearly a waiter she was invisible and so they ignored her.

'I smell treachery!' Pavlov growled. In his case it was an instinctive reaction. When Osmanakhian even hinted at treachery Pavlov salivated in agreement. 'They're listening.'

'They?' asked the first scientist. 'Who's they?'

'They have their bugs everywhere,' his twin brother agreed.

Pavlov grabbed them both by their lapels.

'Just act naturally. Say nothing. What can they know? They can only suspect. But we will keep our lips zippered. We will tell them nothing.'

His female fellow officer and sometime dominatrix, Captain Polina Polinka, had by this time joined the group. She re-iterated the message.

'You will tell them nothing or I will have to whip your little bottom.'

179

But this did not seem to have the intended impact. The first scientist melted under her gaze.

'You little minx, you! I would tell them everything for one of your little lashings.'

Just then Osmanakhian burst into the room.

'I'm suspicious,' he spoke in a clear voice that carried easily. 'I think they may be on to us!'

'They?' Officer Pavlov queried.

Osmanakhian looked at him with disgust.

'Yes, they!' he spoke sharply. 'Not us. We are already on to us. But are they on to us? That is the question. But we are on to them.' His eyes flashed here and there around the room seeking anything to focus on. He saw a file that looked familiar.

'What's that?'

The second scientist looked in the direction Osmanakhian was pointing.

'Oh yes, the plans for the …'

'SSSSssssssh!!!!!'

They all had their fingers to their lips.

'It's just as I feared,' Osmanakhian said strutting round the room. 'They know everything about the …'

Pavlov again put his finger to his lips and Osmanakhian nodding, continued smoothly, without hesitation. 'About the luverly bunch of … of … of?' He wracked his brains for the name of a flower. Then it came to him. 'Daffodils.'

He shook everyone's hand as he repeated the word over and over. 'Daffodils, daffodils.' Then the grim smile on his face slipped into a snarl. 'They're driving me mad! Always listening. Wherever I go. I can never be alone. Their spy planes are hovering overhead. I tell you, it's driving me crazy.'

'Who's always listening?' asked a muffled voice from beneath the bed.

'Who?' Osmanakhian appeared to flounder. 'Who isn't? The Americans, the Russians, the Chinese, the Kazakhs, the Uzbeks.'

'The Uzbeks?' asked the voice again.

'All of them. But I'll show them when the buh ... buh ...' His stuttering was violent.

'Bunch of daffodils,' the voice prompted tentatively.

'Exactly!' Osmanakhian threw his hands into the air. 'When the bunch of daffodils explodes then we shall see where the pretty petals land. Then you will see what kind of man I am ...' He was interrupted at this point by the sound of yapping. 'Fifi? Is that you? Where are you?' His voice was suddenly anguished.

'Now, Fifi! Where are you my little Fifi?' The sound of yapping was eventually found to be coming from behind the bathroom door, where Kono had put the little dog. As soon as the door was open, the dog raced out into Osmanakhian's arms.

'What were you doing in there my little widdly poo-poo?'

But the dog was so severely traumatized it seemed that it couldn't stop yapping and a yellow stream of liquid sprayed across the front of Osmanakhian's uniform.

'Naughty Fifi!' he shouted and waggled the dog in the air with an affectionate laugh.

'Naughty, naughty, silly doggie!'

And then a thought struck him. He whirled round and pointed at the bed. At first there was incomprehension. What did the President mean?

'Under the bed! Fools! There are spies!'

Kono and Ayesha, realizing there was no further point in trying to hide, rolled out from under the bed and stood up. Kono started flexing his legs.

'What are you doing?' Pavlov demanded.

181

'Just testing the floor boards. Making sure they're OK. It seems they are fine.' Kono looked with a straight face at Ayesha.

' How about on your side of the bed?'

Ayesha took the cue and also bounced lightly on her toes.

'I'm not sure about this one. Can you hear the creak?'

Kono appeared to concentrate on the sound.

'No. That's fine. They're all fine. No problem at all. Well, …' he spread out his arms and put on his most appealingly innocent expression. 'I think we had better test the other rooms.' He turned towards the door.

But Osmanakhian, still clutching Fifi, put his hand out to stop him.

'Not so fast!'

He pushed Kono back against the wall.

'You think I don't know who you are? You are FBI or CIA or MI5 or Mossad or SVR or KGB or SAVAK or VEVAK. It's all the same. I will have you tortured. You will confess.'

His spittle sprayed in all directions

'Never!' Kono said bravely but knew that he would break the minute they started to get serious.

'The Chinese water torture!' Osmanakhian screamed.

'Not the water torture!' Ayesha begged.

'We will pull out his nails!'

'Not the nails!' Ayesha begged again.

'We will make you watch BBC for 24 hours.'
'Not the BBC!' Kono himself whimpered.

'Oh yes,' Osmanakhian assured him. 'We will do the BBC torture!' and he laughed demoniacally. 'You will admit everything.'

'OK! OK!' Kono's resolve was gone. 'What do you want to know?'

'Who sent you? Why are you here? What have you found out about …?'

'About what?' Kono asked.

'About … about …' He smacked his forehead. 'Damn you're good!' Osmanakhian glared hard at Kono.

'What are we going to do with you?'

'Feed me to sharks?' Kono suggested.

'That would be a start,' Osmanakhian growled.

Just then the door swung open and three bodyguards tumbled in clutching their heads.

'Fools!' Osmanakhian screamed at them. 'Dolts!'

'Sorry, sir!'

'It won't happen again!'

'You can be sure of that,' the Osmanakhian growl rumbled deeper with threat. Then his eyes widened with surprise. They all looked round to see Solomon carrying in two more bodyguards.

'I'm thinking these are yours, no?' he purred and dropped them on the carpet. Following him into the room were Karl and Mad Mike with Yoshi and Toshi.

'Arrest them!' Osmanakhian screamed and his hands went to his holster, or rather, they went to where the holster would have been if he had been allowed by Customs and Immigration to carry his weapons. At this point, Barnaby sauntered in with his fencing sword twitching menacingly in front of him. Only then did Osmanakhian accept his defeat. He morphed into a snake and hissed just as Freddy appeared to see what all the fuss was about.

'I say. Is everything all right here?' he asked. Snakes? He really was going mad. Still! Stiff upper lip and all that—or whatever it was these limeys said when his back was turned. Soldier on. Shouldn't let a little perceptual lunacy get in the way of such a pleasant afternoon.

Perhaps in recognition of his more elaborated madness, Freddy's appearance had a calming effect on the situation. Kono and Ayesha took advantage of the moment to make their escape, Leona slipping out in their wake. The others formed ranks behind them and engaged in an orderly retreat out of the room down the corridor and down the stairs.

'After them!' they heard Osmanakhian scream and seeing that the bodyguards were re-grouping they knew it was time to make their excuses and run. Jeremiah, who, with Marguerite, had found his way to the roof of the house, jumped on to the branch of a tree and swung gracefully to the lawn. Marguerite, not wishing to be outshone, followed suit hitting the ground with a light, athletic bounce. This was greeted with loud applause by the other guests. Leonardo, hearing the commotion, emerged from behind a bush followed by three girls in various stages of dishevelment.

'Wait!' they screamed. 'Don't go!'

But Leonardo saw it was time to make himself scarce. He ran to the end of the lawn where he found Mad Mike putting the scull into the water. Leonardo helped him and then he himself dived into the river.

Back at the house, Karl found himself cornered momentarily in the pantry by a bodyguard who tried to kick him in the shins. As he hobbled away, clutching his toes, Karl just grinned.

He pulled up his trousers to reveal his metal legs.

'You see? We're not even human. We're aliens.'

The bodyguard's eyes opened wide in terror and he fainted. Karl stepped over his body and departed by the back door.

❧

All the athletes were busy making their way to the car where

Perkins was standing with the door open. Lord Haverstock surprised everybody by felling a bodyguard with a kung fu kick.

'You are my hero!' Anna whispered to him as he ushered her into the car. Jade whirled head over heels in a series of cartwheels across the flower beds and then over half a dozen car roofs before somersaulting to the ground beside Perkins. One after the other they got into the car.

'Is everyone here?' Barnaby asked as he closed the door behind him.

'What about Ivan?' Yoshi asked and everyone was surprised. Until now he had not spoken a word. They had assumed he couldn't speak English.

'Yes, Ivan. He's not here,' said Toshi and everyone looked to him too in surprise.

'You speak English?'

'Of course!' they said in unison and shook their heads at each other that anyone could have thought differently.

Looking out of the car window they could see Ivan approaching, riding on Marla's back. She was running gamely as he whipped her buttocks. Behind them, the basketball team were passing balls between them and generally interfering with the enemy's progress. One after the other they all too got into the car. Except for Marla. She passed her card in through the open window to Ivan.

'You will ring me, won't you?'

Ivan gave her a thumbs up but Marla was not convinced.

'They all say that,' she muttered to no-one in particular as she wiped her eyes. But this was no time for long sad scenes of departure. Perkins hopped into the driver's seat and the Rolls slowly moved off down the drive. The bodyguards caught up with them and started to bang on the sides and roof. A window opened and a smoke bomb was hurled out into their midst. It was a peculiarly pinkish and pungent smelling smoke and the bodyguards were soon clutching their throats and trying to stem the tears that flowed from their eyes as they heard, but could not see, the sound of the car recede.

'Oh I say!' Freddy said having just caught up with them. 'I wish they didn't have to go! This was the best garden party ever!'

4.

Twenty minutes later, the doubt that had been curdling gently in Barnaby's gut began to thicken. He looked round at all the athletes in the car and counted them off. No doubt about it, except for Leonardo and Mad Mike, they were all present and then there was Anna and Lord Haverford. They too were in the car. But it seemed to him that somehow, somewhere, somewho, something was not quite right. There was an absence—a very definite absence. What could it be? And then it hit him. That man Jones. The poet. They'd left their host behind. There was only one thing for it.

'Perkins!'

'Sir?'

'Jones. The poet.'

'Yes sir?'

'We've left him behind.'

'Ah!' Perkins said thoughtfully. 'I see!' Always quick on the uptake was Perkins.

'What are we going to do?'

'Just a minute, sir.'

There was a lay-by just up ahead and Perkins eased the Rolls off the road. He extracted a slim mobile phone from an inside pocket and pressed a number of buttons before putting it to his ear. There was complete silence in the car as everyone tried to work out what was going on.

'Mr Fruhmanhoff? ... Yes, this is Perkins. I don't know if you remember ... Ah good! Yes, perfectly fine ... Yes, I'm glad to say he's much better ... Yes, I see! ... And how is the garden party going? ... Good! Good! ... Well, now. I was wondering if you could do me a little favour ... you see. Mr Jones the well known ex-poet laureate of the Olympic Games ... A smallish man, rumpled suit, last seen admiring paintings on the first floor of your house ...'

❧

Rowan Jones was indeed at that very moment looking at a painting that if he didn't know better looked exactly like an original Gauguin. He knew better though simply because the cost of an original Gauguin made it unimaginably unlikely that this was one. That much he knew. His champagne befuddled mind was not that befuddled. There was a stirring behind him and the elegant woman stretched out on the bed began to stir. Rowan Jones watched her with the still fascination of a scientist. In a moment she was going to open her eyes and find herself in a bedroom with a complete stranger. And then she was going to ...? Rowan's hypothesis was that she was going to scream blue murder and that he was going to have a very awkward time trying to explain himself. A task made more difficult as he couldn't quite remember where he was. All he knew was that the champagne was excellent. So it was with some surprise that he found her suddenly wide eyed and looking around with a smile.

'Such a pleasant dream,' she said.

'Was it?' Rowan was happy to lead her along the path of remembrance.

'I was walking across a lake in the middle of a volcano that was set in a vast ocean. The sky was raining flower petals and then a canoe approached, paddled by four dark muscular men—such handsome men. And I sat in the canoe with them and they transported me towards a place where a waterfall plunged down into a deep clear pool where golden fish swirled and the air was filled with the song of a thousand song birds.' She was clearly entranced with the images in her brain.

She held out her hand.

'Come here.' She patted the bed beside her and Rowan rose to do her bidding. But how this scene might have unfolded we shall never know because at that precise moment the door swung open and Osmanakhian strode in followed by Major Pavlov and three burly bodyguards.

'There!' Osmanakhian screamed with barely restrained hysteria. 'That man!'

Rowan Jones had a strong sense of imminent claustrophobia, of an oppressive shrinking of perspectives. He found himself, rather strangely, wondering what to do with his hands. There was a window behind him but it was closed and he knew there was no possibility of escape in that direction. He was not the kind of person who would throw himself out of a window without having given great thought to what would happen next. He noted the heavy metal objects that the guards were fitting to their knuckles. On the other hand he was not the sort of person who waited to see what kind of violence they could inflict upon him. Or maybe he was, he thought, with that passive resignation that seemed to go hand in hand with half a bottle of very good champagne. Maybe he should shout 'help!' The others would be bound to hear him. Yes, where were the others? But even as he was thinking this, the guards started to move towards him. 'Ooooh!' he thought. This was going to be tricky. Perhaps the woman would save him. They wouldn't want to do anything violent in front of her, would they? Not in front of a lady. A First Lady to boot. He looked at her in hope but saw her eyes were alight with expectant pleasure. 'Oooh!' he thought a little more loudly this time. How was he going to get out of this? Suddenly there was a disturbance in the smooth flow of inevitability. A new presence at the doorway. Everyone turned to see who it was.

'Oh! I say.' Freddy oozed charming ineffectiveness. 'Has anyone seen a Welsh poet chappie?'

There was a long pause as everyone tried to work out what the next step was.

'Very important to get him home. Got a helicopter waiting.'

'Yes,' Rowan croaked, his voice dry with terror and fearful hope. 'That's me.'

❧

Back in the car, there was a strained silence. No-one was prepared to challenge the firm clarity of Perkins' raised finger. The minutes ticked by. Trucks thundered by. It was not such a wide lay-by that they were divorced from the onward march of the day. Then the phone rang.

'Perkins here,' said Perkins. Then after some intense listening, he smiled.

'Thank *you*, Mr Fruhmanhoff.' And for the first time he allowed himself a quiet smile of satisfaction as he gave a thumbs up to show all was well. When the call was ended, Perkins switched off the phone and returned it to his jacket pocket.

'An explanation, Perkins?' Barnaby's voice was quivering with a barely suppressed, ever so slightly brittle, irritation.

'Sir?'

'What are you doing with Freddy Fruhmanhoff's personal phone number?'

Perkins was aware of a general craning of necks. Everyone, it seemed, wanted to know.

'He gave it to me, sir.' There was a pause as he waited for a gap in the stream of traffic before once again pulling out into the road heading west towards the Welsh hills.

'And why would Mr Fruhmanhoff of the New York Fruhmanhoff's wish to encourage discourse with someone such as yourself?' There was a definite peeved quality to the repressed outrage.

'Not long ago I was in the position of being able to do Mr Fruhmanhoff a favour. Something of a personal nature. Naturally I can't go into any details given the sensitivity of the subject but it involved two actors from Hollywood who, unknown to themselves, required rescuing from a bevy, I think you might call it, of girls from the Folies Bergère who were themselves being used as a decoy by a group of renegade Israelis, Mossad defectors as it happened who were in cahoots with the liberal wing of Hamas and were intending to put pressure, in a roundabout sort of way, on the Polish salt mines directorate—and this is where it got entangled with Fruhmanhoff interests. Somehow, along the way, a nephew of mine found himself involved and asked me to do some mediating, which I am glad to say I was able to do to general satisfaction all round. Mr Freddy Fruhmanhoff expressed great gratitude and said if there was ever anything I needed, he would be glad to ...'

A great silence filled the car. It was the silence of a profound contemplation on the complex interweaving of fates.

As the helicopter took off from the helipad behind the house, Rowan Jones looked down at the building, and more specifically at the maze beside it. He marvelled at the intricate interleaving of hedge and the complexity of the pattern. It was a fiendish labyrinth. A trap for the unwary. It gave him the willies. The heebie-jeebies. The jitters. The almighty jim-jams. The very idea of being lost in a place like that .... He shuddered at the thought. And then he saw the man, right in the heart of the coil, who, if he was not mistaken, looked very like one of the bodyguards, it seemed, a man who was curled up in a ball and screaming the scream of the mad. But perhaps he was mistaken.

He only caught a glimpse before the helicopter suddenly lurched up and away, and the house and the maze and the lawns grew smaller and smaller, and then they were gone from sight, and the patchwork that is England spread itself below them. Fields and roads and from time to time a village or even a town passed below them. Rowan raised the bottle of champagne to his lips but was disappointed to find nothing left. The pilot pointed to a handle next to Rowan's seat. Pulling it, Rowan was pleased to discover that it was attached to a refrigerated compartment in which nestled another bottle. He managed to uncork the bottle without causing mayhem in the cockpit and finding a rack of glasses, he poured himself a generous portion. Only then did he sit back and relax. Really, life couldn't be any better, he thought. And then he remembered the bomb.

5.

It was late at the farmhouse. Rowan arrived home first giving Bronwyn the surprise of her life when he stepped out of the helicopter. She had gone out to hurl vituperation at whoever it was that was disturbing the rabbits and cats and pigs and chickens and ducks and dogs and all the rest of the animals with this satanic chagga-chagga-chagga of the helicopter's rotor motor. Only to find, to her great surprise—though her capacity for surprise was very much reduced these last few weeks—that the man stepping out of the infernal machine was her very own husband.

'How?' she waved her arms.

But the champagne bottle in the one hand and the glass in the other explained very clearly why he was unable to give a clear account of events. So, once the helicopter had gone, she led him to his bed and took his shoes off and laid him down to dream of lakes in volcanoes and showers of flower petals and handsome men rowing canoes to waterfalls. It was a very pleasant dream. Though it would have been very much pleasanter if he had been alone, if there hadn't been some appalling woman disporting herself in a somewhat robustly rude way—she seemed vaguely familiar for some reason—and doing impertinent things to a little dog called Fifi.

Some time later, he heard the Rolls draw up to the door. Looking out the window he saw that the evening had taken on a pearly translucence. His head was clear as a bell and he was ready for action. He waved to everyone as they emerged from the car.

Later, after dinner, they were all discussing the day's events.

'There's no doubt about it,' Marguerite insisted. 'The bomb is going to explode at exactly ten past four tomorrow afternoon.'

'Where?'

She shrugged.

'That's all I heard.'

'We should tell the police,' Rowan suggested but then saw the futility of it. 'Why should they believe us? The whole story is crazy!'

No-one spoke as they all pondered the matter.

'But we can't just do nothing!'

They all looked at each other and there was much shrugging and shaking of heads.

'Perhaps,' said Perkins. 'If I might be so bold, I'd like to suggest that each of us thinks back on the day's events and see if we can remember any detail, no matter how small, that might be significant.'

'Perkins is right,' Rowan was the first to respond. 'I'll start. Let me see now. I was in one room, before I found the room with the fake Gauguin, there was a bedroom where of all things they had a couple of dozen replica Olympic torches.' He laughed. 'The silly souvenirs people buy!' He grinned.

'Of course!' The implication was immediately obvious to them all—all, that is, except Rowan. Finally, even he understood.

'Oh my God! Of course! The torches! They're going to put a bomb in the Olympic torch and when they light the Olympic flame the whole thing is going to explode. That's it! We've got to tell the police.'

'If I may make another suggestion,' Perkins spoke with quiet earnestness. 'I think I have a better idea.'

Part Five

1.

'The Olympic flame will start the final stretch of its journey at 10.30 am here at Wembley, where it has been kept overnight.' Perkins pointed his stick at the map of London they had painstakingly sellotaped to the wall. 'Then it will follow this route down Ladbroke Grove to Notting Hill Gate. From there it will proceed along to Oxford Street and to Charing Cross Road. Then it will go down to the river, looping round Trafalgar Square and then along the river bank to St Paul's Cathedral. From there, it's a straight run through Whitechapel to the new Olympic stadium in Stratford. Let's look at the timings. It will arrive at the stadium at five past four.' Perkins looked at all the faces staring intently on the map.

'They definitely said that the bomb was due to go off at ten past four.' Marguerite's voice was low with concern.

'That means they are waiting for the crucial moment when the eyes of the world will be focused on the flame. This is the psychological moment. An explosion now would ...' All around the room heads were nodding in comprehension. It was clear to all of them that this was one bomb that mustn't be allowed to explode.

'I think it is safe to say that security will be very tight.' Perkins wrapped his stick against the map. 'At some time there will be a switch.'

'But each link on the relay has its own torch. Only the flame is passed on from one runner to the next.' It was Bronwyn who somehow knew this detail.

'So the exchange will probably be the last exchange.' There was a pause as they all considered this. 'But maybe not. They might have any number of tricks up their sleeve. Maybe there will be more than one bomb. Our job is to make sure there are no bomb explosions. For that reason we will have to shadow the torch relay for much of the way.'

There were grim nods.

'So. Get some sleep. We've got an early start tomorrow.'

Perkins could have been a squadron leader sending his fighter pilots into battle. Everyone obeyed his instructions unthinkingly. They had grown accustomed to their bunks of straw in the barn and outhouses of the farm. Within fifteen minutes they were all curled up in their beds and fast asleep. All except Perkins who still had arrangements to make.

2.

The next morning they set off from the farmhouse early. Bronwyn had got up even earlier to bake the buns they ate for breakfast and prepare the coffee they washed them down with. They emerged from the Welsh hills into the undulating farmlands of middle England. Here they merged with the steady streams of early morning motorway traffic that took them at a steady seventy to eighty miles an hour towards London and their destiny. Would they be able to thwart the plan? The consequences of failure were unthinkable.

❧

It was already ten o'clock when the pink Rolls drew up to the side of the road behind a large white van in the exclusive Holland Park area of London. There were several other smaller vehicles nearby and a small huddle of drivers stood by the cab of the white van smoking and chatting. Perkins got out of the car to greet them.

'Henry!' he greeted a young man warmly. 'And these are your friends?'

'Yes, this here is …' Henry started to do the introductions but Perkins put his hand on his arm.

'Not now, Henry, if you don't mind. Hopefully we'll all have time later on to get to know each other but time is pressing.'

'Right you are Uncle Sid.' Then, before Perkins could stop him, he turned to his friends and boasted in a loud voice.

'This here is my Uncle Sid. Best caser of a country house you'll ever meet. Why three years ago …'

'Not now, dear boy. Another time.'

But the damage was done

'Three years ago?' Barnaby murmured, having heard everything. 'That wouldn't have been the Mainmarch Estate by any chance?'

'Yes.' Henry had not yet grasped the situation. 'That was it!'

'Henry!' Perkins voice was sharp. 'I said enough!'

'Ooops!' Henry saw his mistake too late. 'Have I put my foot in it?'

'Neighbours of mine, as it happens.' Barnaby continued. 'In fact, come to think of it, all my neighbours have been,' he paused. 'What's the term? Done over? Turned over? Anyway they've all been burgled. Mine's the only house so far to have escaped.' He gave Perkins a hard look. 'I wonder why?'

Perkins shrugged. 'One should never—how should I put it?—urinate in one's own flower bed.'

'Quite!'

'Anyway,' Perkins took a hurried look at his watch. 'I think we should leave this discussion for another time. We have work to do.'

Henry opened up the van doors. Inside there was a great deal of electronic equipment and a large screen. Henry flipped a switch and suddenly they could all see the opening ceremonies being televised. And then, before their eyes, a runner held aloft the Olympic torch and started the long run out of the stadium and on to the streets of London.

'Check your watches gentlemen! It is now exactly ten thirty.'

Everyone set their watch to that time.

'We can't afford any mistakes.' Perkins was standing in the van addressing the athletes and the men his nephew, Henry, had assembled. 'This van will be the command centre. Everyone else will be divided up into teams. Our job is to monitor the progress of the torch through the city. Now let's sort out the teams and what we want them to do.'

3.

An hour later. Perkins and Barnaby were watching the events on the screen in the back of the van. The flame was being passed from one runner to another. Each runner carried the torch for half a mile and then holding the torches together passed on the flame to the next runner. Some way behind the runner it was possible to see two women on bicycles among the following crowd.

'Good. Ayesha and Leona are in position.'

Perkins put on a set of ear-phones and twiddled the knobs on a black box.

'Ayesha. Can you read me?'

'Read you?' came the voice loud and clear. 'I don't know if I can read you but I can hear you if that's what you mean.'

'Excellent. What's happening?'

'Nothing so far. It's not so easy for me to go so slowly. But everything is normal so far.'

Perkins gave Barnaby a thumbs up sign to show all was well.

'It's the waiting, Perkins, that I can't stand.' Barnaby had his hands firmly pocketed. 'It's this damnable waiting.'

'Indeed sir. The quiet before the storm.'

'About these robberies, Perkins, …' he thought to pass the time by enquiring further into the cleaning out of several large mansions close to his own but Perkins held up his hand sharply to silence him. Ayesha was talking again.

'Something's happening!'

Looking at the screen, they could see what she was talking about. A dozen or so runners, all carrying torches, had joined the main runner.

'They're all carrying torches!' she said, stating the obvious.

'Stay with the main runner!' Perkins instructed but suddenly the radio link went dead. Instinctively they looked at the screen and just caught sight of a cyclist being knocked to the ground.

'Ayesha! Ayesha! Are you there?'

But there was no response.

Leona had seen the fist emerge from the crowd and strike Ayesha. Without thinking she hurled herself on the man and smashed her fists into his face.

'Bastard!'

The crowd around her who had witnessed everything burst into applause but no-one else seemed at all inclined to intervene. Then Leona thought of Ayesha and made her way to her friend who was gingerly picking herself off the ground.

'Are you OK my sweet?' she asked and unable to stop herself, bent down to kiss the bruises. (Ah! What heady perfume! What bliss it would be to have a night of love.)

'Really, I'm fine. I'm OK.' Ayesha struggled to her feet. Leona was a sweetie but she was beginning to feel oppressed by her constant presence. Still, at a time like this it was good she was there to give her a hand. Together they moved their bikes to the side of the road. Their assailant too went off rubbing his jaw.

Not so very far away, as the crow flies, another van was parked by the side of the road. The official runner found himself being pushed by the other runners towards it. Much as he struggled to stay in the centre of the lane there was no avoiding the fact that he was being diverted. As he approached, the van doors opened wide and he was bustled into the back of the van. None of this appeared on the television screen. The camera had been tricked into following one of the other runners who proceeded to the next hand-over point where he passed his flame to the waiting female athlete. As soon as the flame had been transferred, she was off. And, as she was an attractive girl, the camera was pleased to follow her. Now that the Olympic flame had passed, the crowd dispersed. When everyone had gone, the van slowly pulled out and drove off. In the front passenger seat there was a woman who looked very like a certain army officer in the Transcaucasian elite division, an officer called Captain Polina Polinka, and on her lap a dog that she called Fifi. In the back of the van was an extremely frightened athlete with a gun pointed at his head.

Perkins shook his head at Barnaby.

'I think, sir, we can assume they're making the switch as we speak!'

'But what about the girls?'

'Don't worry about them.' It was Henry who spoke. 'We've got their location on the GPS. We'll get them picked up in no time.'

'But I don't understand. What was that all about?'

'He's passed on a false flame.'

'So? Is that such a big deal, Perkins?'

'Not to you or me, sir. To us, it's just a spectacle. But to someone who takes the symbolism seriously then it is a big deal. It means that the Olympics will be accompanied by a false flame.'

'But no-one will know.'

'The perpetrator will know. Maybe he's recorded it. Maybe when the Olympics are well under way he will release the news to the press. It's one way to undermine the Olympics—if that's what he wants to do.'

'So what are we going to do about it?'

Perkins picked up the microphone and flipped a switch

to open all communication channels simultaneously.

'The flame has been switched. All systems go! Repeat. All systems go!'

~

Three miles away, close to the centre of the city, Jeremiah was enjoying being the centre of attention as passers-by gawped at him astride a Harley hog with a very bored but exotic looking Marguerite sitting on the back. In fact she was not at all bored but the attitude sat on her with the force of habit. They were parked at the side of a Soho street waiting for instructions. Jeremiah was studying a map of London's main streets trying to get a sense of the layout of the city. Give him a tropical jungle any day.

'Your American so-called rugged individualism is really just the same as our French existentialism,' Marguerite commented, having decided that a little light conversation was required to pass the time.

'That so?' He didn't pay her any attention.

'So basically we have the same attitude to life,' she persevered.

'Yeah?'

'Yes. We both believe in the integrity and priority of the individual's personal dynamic in constructing contexts and objectives.'

'I just live on my own and hunt deer and rabbits and anything else I can get a hold of,' he drawled. 'I don't go in for any of that integrity and priority stuff.' He laughed. 'You know what's wrong with you?'

'There is something wrong with me?' her tone made it clear she was ready for battle.

'Yeah. You think too much. You use too many words. You need a man to give you a …'

'I know what you want to give me.' She spat derisively. 'And who do you give it to when you're up there in your lonely cabin in the mountains? Hein? To your goats?'

Just where this conversation was going will never be known because at that moment there was a buzz from the walkie-talkie and Marguerite put the ear-phones on.

'Yes?' she asked into the mouth piece. 'OK! Go! It's go? OK. We go.'

Jeremiah had already kicked the Harley's motor into life.

'Hold on now,' he called out as he pulled out into the traffic.

'Let's go get those suckers.'

Thick crowds lined the route. Everyone enjoys being part of history. For the old it was a long awaited dream. For the young it was an experience they would be able to tell their grandchildren. The Olympics don't come to London every day. In Trafalgar Square crowd density was if anything even greater. In part this was because of the enormous screen that had been set up. On a podium next to it stood Catherine Zeta-Jones. She was giving her breathless commentary as events unfolded on the screen. For some reason it isn't enough to see what we see; we need to be told what it is we are watching — preferably by an extremely attractive woman. And as if this scene was not enough in itself, it too had to be filmed and commented on from a studio so that people who had decided to share this breathless national moment from the comfort of their own sofas could do so knowing that they weren't missing anything except the inconvenience of the physical press of bodies. Thank God there were tourists who didn't have homes they could watch this from.

'What a day this is,' Catherine, with her usual

professionalism, glossed the national mood. 'What a momentous occasion. The Olympics are finally coming to London once again, What a celebration of sport and athleticism we are in for. And here comes the Olympic flame itself ...'

The screen showed an athlete running along a street seemingly running on the spot so extreme was the perspective offered by the long range camera lens. His hands held the white torch. His face was grim with the awe of knowing he was bearing the proud celestial flame that had come all the way from the Olympic grotto in Olympia. What he probably didn't know was that it was Hitler himself who had instituted the long journey of the flame to add to the mystique of the 1936 games. But everyone likes a bit of mystique, a slice of portentous theatre. None more than our dear Catherine who was bravely adding her ad libbed commentary.

'Here comes the flame. Proud symbol of peace and friendship for a mightily proud occasion. We are taking part in a truly historic moment.'

Catherine's research notes here carried a great deal of data about the torch that she could—with nonchalance and practiced ease insinuate into the commentary. For example, the torch has come overland from Greece and in order to maximize the number of countries, especially the new members of the European Union, it had taken a circuitous route through the Balkans, Romania, Bulgaria, Hungary, Slovakia, the Czech Republic, Austria, Italy, Switzerland, France, Germany, the Netherlands, Belgium and finally by sea to England. The torch itself was a complex design having two flames—one yellow, visible to the passing crowds but sadly exposed to wind and rain and therefore in danger of being put out; the other a carefully cosseted blue flame that was used to relight the torch should that need ever occur. As if the flame was a thing in itself, rather than a spectrum of light and heat emitted by the burning materials—but Catherine's research notes do not contain this sacrilegious, heretical, but self-evident truth. We are in the world of symbol and myth. This Olympian fire was lit by the action of mirrors (yes, it's all done with mirrors!)—lit by actresses playing the part of ancient Greek priestesses at the site of the ancient games, yes, at Olympia itself. And this is somehow perfectly symbolic of the entire edifice of symbol and make believe. The runners too are actors in a game as are the spectators. Everyone pretending that the importance of the occasion was, well, somehow important. From Olympia the flame was taken first to Athens and from there it was carried by a relay of runners—men and women—across the landmass of Europe. Catherine tells of the 2,964 miles that the torch has been carried on its journey, the fact that it is made of aluminium, that it weighs less than one kilo. That 19,465 torches have been required. And all the while we see the runners bobbing their way along the city streets, one after the other, getting closer (that at least is the inference).

'How are we going to rescue the flame, Perkins?' Barnaby was not of the sort who take symbols lightly. He was concerned too with the reputation of his games. Yes, *his* games. He did not want them to go down in history with its reputation sullied.

'That is already in hand sir. Our friends Jeremiah and Marguerite have been given their task. Now, our job is to slow things down a little.'

'Slow things down? Whatever for?'

But before Perkins could explain the walkie-talkie buzzed and he pressed the switch to receive the call.

'Yes,' he said. 'Yes, we need to interfere. Do what you can.'

Then he replaced the hand set. For several minutes

neither of them said anything. Then Barnaby held up a placating hand tentatively.

'I appreciate that this is not the time nor the place to discuss the matters such as the Mainmarch Estate break in. I just want to say that when you are ready to talk I might very well be interested in a piece of the action. I think that's the phrase I'm looking for.'

'A piece of the action?' Perkins asked, his face refusing to give anything away as to the emotions he might, or might not, be feeling.

'Just a thought,' Barnaby murmured. 'I've had one or two ideas.'

༝

Yoshi and Toshi had chosen to dress in large green plaid suits with black shoes with white spats. On their heads they wore bowler hats. It was, in its way, their homage to Britain. Yoshi carried a walking stick and Toshi had a camera — an Olympus, as it happened. The runner was still two hundred yards from their position when Toshi ordered Yoshi into the middle of the road to have his photo taken. Then another photo and a third. Yoshi posed himself as a dandy, as a clown, as a tap dancer, as a fool. Toshi made a great fuss about the poses and the effort of setting up each shot diverted the spectators. There was a lot of laughter to which the twins responded by bowing this way and that with long sweeping bows such as a gallant cavalier might make. And all the time the athlete was approaching with the no-longer Olympian flame.

The athlete in question was big Jack McBerry, a putter of the shot and a hurler of the discus for his athletic club, the Hackney Hammers. He was not therefore fleet of foot. But he was built of solid muscle. Jack's experience of life, both on and off the athletics track was that when he approached, other people tended to get out of the way. Jack also knew from his schooldays that the shortest distance between two points was a straight line and he had no intention of deviating in the slightest, no matter what. This was a proud day for Jack McBerry, one that he had every intention of talking about at regular intervals throughout the rest of his life—and if you didn't want to listen you knew what you could do with yourself. So Jack McBerry padded slowly along the road towards what at first he had assumed to be a mirage, and then one of those street entertainments that the council must have put on to entertain the crowds until he came along for them to ooh and aaah and generally ogle—because Jack McBerry knew he was the main attraction for this section of the route and he had no intention of sharing this moment of exposure and let's face it, fame, with any twat who happened to be in the way.

But as he approached closer he could see that whoever it was that was in his way had no intention of getting out of it. The spectators had by now seen the situation and were one and all shouting at Yoshi and Toshi to get out of the way, to move, to see what was thundering their way. But the more people yelled and pointed, the more Yoshi and Toshi appeared to be bemused, bewildered, and confused, and the more firmly they blocked the line of progress, shrugging and talking to each other, making extravagant gestures with their hands and arms. And Jack McBerry steamed ever closer. Finally, at the last minute, they turned and Jack found himself confronted by the two twins who feinted this way and that—and while he was focusing on one, the other smacked his arm sharply in a way that caused his hand to open. Before he knew what was happening, the torch had been snatched out of his hand. It took Jack another five paces before he realized he was no longer carrying the torch and another five to stop and turn. By this time the spectators were roaring with guilty laughter as Toshi snapped away at Yoshi who was posing with the torch: standing with it, kneeling with it, flexing his legs with it.

'Hoi!' This just wasn't on. Jack was not going to stand for this.

He dashed towards Yoshi with the intention of breaking him in two and extracting from his fingers the aluminium torch but it didn't quite work out like that. As Jack McBerry plunged on in his going forward trajectory, Yoshi, while simultaneously seeming to stand firm, appeared to melt around him so that they exchanged locational data without coming into physical contact with each other. The spectators took it for a magic act and they all clapped. When Jack managed to seize Yoshi's wrists—an act he appeared to achieve only with the connivance of Yoshi himself—it was only to find that it was now Toshi who had a grip on the torch.

Two miles away, watching these events on the screen in Trafalgar Square, Catherine Douglas (nee Zeta Jones) was desperately trying to keep up a respectable flow of words.

'There appears to be an uh … unauthorized interruption to the schedule. The schedule is very tight and every single detail has been timed and planned to cover every eventuality. Except, perhaps for this eventuality.'

There was a great gasp as Jack McBerry first caught hold of Toshi's arm but then almost immediately found himself doing a backward somersault. Fortunately Yoshi was there to break the fall or he might have hurt himself. Both Yoshi and Toshi then pulled him to his feet, turned him in the direction he should be going, handed him the torch and gave him a gentle push. As Jack McBerry padded away from them he heard a titter from the crowd. He couldn't see that Yoshi and Toshi had simply bowed together in his direction. They meant this as a formal gesture to show respect for an honourable foe. They certainly did not mean this as a joke or an affront but sadly the spectators took it to have ironic significance and they did titter.

Half a mile further on, Jack's successor with the torch, Selene Laing-Khan, long jumper from Bradford, found herself confronted by a man who had, or so it appeared, replaced his legs with springs. He was springing and spronging all along the route and unfortunately did not seem to have proper control over his equipment so she had to slow down and finally stop as he made up his mind which way he intended to bounce. He indicated that he was not in control and apologized mutely with his arms. She tried to go round but whenever she made a move he did too. It was bad form, she knew (this had been instilled from a very early age) for the able bodied to exert physical primacy over the physically disabled. But much as she appealed to the crowd, they simply laughed at her predicament.

Catherine Zeta Jones, one and half miles away in Trafalgar Square, watched on her vast screen as some man—dressed like a deranged puppet—bounced around in the road forcing the female athlete (she consulted her notes and hoped she was right to refer to her as Lindsay Althorpe-Cousins, swimmer for the Edinburgh Penguins team) to come to a standstill. Catherine was at a loss as to whether she should take an amused stance—or to be angry and outraged, and if the latter whether she should do so on behalf of the Olympic Games Organizing Committee, or the People of Great Britain and Northern Ireland. She searched her notes in vain for any indication that these interruptions had been officially sanctioned—that they were indeed part of the official entertainment on offer.

❧

Lord Coe was at the Olympic Stadium with the other members

of the Organising Committee and many tens of thousands of people who had paid good money to attend the opening ceremonies, not to mention the many invited heads of state. They were all watching Catherine's broadcast on the screens of the stadium itself.

He consulted his watch. His assistant was talking energetically into a microphone attached to his ear as he twirled a dial deftly with his right thumb. 'Just a minute,' the man said and leaned towards Lord Coe.

'Interruptions.' He murmured.

'I can see that!' Lord Coe was grimly aware that camera were trained on him at all times and he was damned if he was going to appear in the front pages the next day with a worried furrow on his visage.

'Looks like we're running ten minutes late so far.'

So be it, Lord Coe muttered to himself and smiled a smile of grim, photogenic geniality at Angela Merkel, the German Chancellor, and he let the smile embrace with glacial amicability the man sitting next to her, the rather bizarre dictator of Transcaucasia—what was his name? Not that it mattered. He had long since learned the art of avoiding names. And in any case the man was deeply involved in a conversation on his cell phone. He was throwing his arms around—to the more than slight irritation of the Merkels. He would have to learn to behave better than that if he expected to join the European Union anytime soon. Perhaps he should have seated him next to Signor Berlusconi. Too late now, of course. Signor Berlusconi had come with his entire cabinet— twenty eight very attractive women. Only in Italy, Lord Coe sighed with an amusement saturated with envy. 'Berl's Babes' the tabloids were calling them. But the lack of security was an icicle of concern. How were these bizarre people being allowed to disrupt the smooth progress of the torch?

President Osmanakhian was also concerned at the delays to the progress of the torch. He had placed a rather large bet (at odds of 73/1) on the possibility that there might be an explosion within the Olympic stadium between four and four twenty. But now? The torch containing the bomb was ready and waiting in a small white van parked about half a mile from the stadium—the same van that contained the gagged and bound athlete who had been stripped of his shoes, shorts and tracksuit top. His replacement had put them on and was ready to go. Now it was just a matter of substituting one runner for another. They had done it once, now they had to repeat it. The other runners were in a second van parked a few hundred yards further away. But they couldn't go until the official runner had passed them—and something was going wrong with the timing. The bloody English could never get the timings right. Their train service was the laughing stock of the entire world. How on earth had they expected to get the timings of the torch relay right? And now President Osmanakhian was going berserk. Well it wasn't their fault. What did he want them to do? Start running now and make a complete hash of it?

And in another van, Perkins and Barnaby St John Smythe were watching the screen, also with some concern.

'What do you think the big plan is, Perkins?'

'Well sir, the torch relay is a diversion. Obviously, there has to be another substitution. That will have to happen just before the end. Whoever is the last athlete in the relay will have to have his torch changed. That's what we've got to stop happening.'

'How on earth are we going to do that?'

'Well, what would happen if we hijacked the torch?'

'Hijacked it?'

'Yes, if we hijacked the torch in front of all the cameras,

in front of the eyes of the whole world, then the torch relay would be completely disrupted. It couldn't be allowed to continue.'

'I'm not sure I follow, Perkins.'

'If the torch relay doesn't reach the stadium then the plan to substitute the last torch will be thrown into disarray.'

'And the reputation of the London Olympics will go up with a bang. Come on, Perkins. We simply can't allow that to happen.'

'Well, I've arranged for a little bit of theatre that might just save the day.'

'Theatre, Perkins?' The St John Smythe eyebrow quivered quizzically with a strong suggestion of disapproval.

❧

Catherine Zeta Jones was once again commentating. The relay was now back on track, albeit several minutes behind schedule. The runners were approaching St Paul's Cathedral and she had a whole screed of information to impart on that important edifice—how it was the master work of that great architect, Sir Christopher Wren, and how it was completed exactly three hundred years ago (well actually three hundred and two years ago). And how it survived the heavy bombing of the East End of London during the last war (best not say *German* bombers, she told herself. now that we were all partners in the great enterprise called Europe—and everyone understood which war was the last one—all these other silly wars since then not really counting as true wars.).

'Here she comes. What a proud moment this is. In a minute she will turn the corner and find herself face to face with the building that perhaps more than any other defines what it means to be British. Built in ...' Catherine was just about to launch into her carefully prepared potted lecture when she saw on the screen a big burly, bearded man with the small head covering that so clearly stated his Jewishness step out into the road and abruptly extract the torch from the athlete's surprised fingers. When she tried to grab it back he simply held out his hand and kept her at bay. A second man, a lean African, gleaming black, stepped out into the road, took the torch from the first man and started running towards the river. A number of mounted police had been deployed at this junction of several wide streets. Seeing the commotion the police officer closest to the scuffle started to force his horse through the crowds to intercept the man with the torch.

'Good!' Perkins exclaimed. 'Kono has the torch. Now he just needs to stay ahead of the police horse.'

But it was clear that the mounted policeman was going to cut him off. But just as Kono found himself cornered, pressed against the side of a building by the horse, a Chinese girl slipped under the horse's belly and took the torch. Back under the belly she went. The horse reared at the sudden, unwelcome warmth of the flame. Jade cart-wheeled across the space in front of her, the policeman fought to control his mount. That achieved he set off after her. A wild-eyed man had climbed up a nearby statue pedestal. As the policeman passed close by, he leapt and quickly replaced him, bundling the policeman to the ground. Then, snatching the torch that Jade held up to him, Ivan—for it is he—spurred the horse down the narrow lane that leads to the pedestrian Millennium Bridge. Behind him there was a melee as the other mounted police charged down the lane after him. Ivan smiled knowing they would never catch him. All he needed was the fifty yard start that he had. As the horse's hooves clanged loud on the metallic surface of the bridge itself, tourists flung themselves out of the way.

'Yaaaay!!!' he screamed forgetting for a moment where

he was. Then, half way across the bridge, he pulled his horse up and turned to his pursuers. They too brought their mounts to a halt. In the brief silence that enveloped them, before anyone had the wits to speak, Ivan stood up in his stirrups and sent the torch whirling into the air. Everyone watched aghast as the torch spun in the clear light of this, until now, perfect day. The sky was a cloudless blue. The river a flat grey. The only sound was the honking of a seagull. Otherwise the river was seemingly deserted. The torch fell out of sight below the horizon of the parapet. A second later there was the sound of an explosion and a plume of water erupted high into the air.

'Bomb!' said Ivan. 'We save you from the bomb!'

No microphone was able to pick up the words but the cameras had recorded everything and as the long range telephoto lenses zeroed in on Ivan it was obvious from his gestures that he was telling the police he had saved the relay from a tragic disaster.

Inside the stadium, there were gasps and shrieks of horror as the whole incident was played and replayed again and again in slow motion on the screens above the crowd. Lord Coe was oblivious now to the cameras taking his photo. There was no shame in appearing shocked when confronted by shocking events. Somehow a team of circus clowns—this was how they appeared to him to be—had saved countless innocent by-standers from being blown to smithereens. They were heroes. But who were they and how had they known about the plot? The clarity of events was dissolving into a quagmire of murky possibilities—the maggoty pond mud of reality.

As Ivan allowed himself to be taken into custody—it was entirely a matter of his deciding to allow it, to suppress for a moment the terrible pride of the Rimsky-Radetskis, which he did for the sake of his host, and of his team and for the plan itself because if he did not allow himself to be taken into custody then the police might take it into their heads to investigate further beneath the arch of the bridge. And if they did that they would find a scull there—and in the scull a man who might still have the residues of explosive materials on his fingers.

≈

'How on earth …?' Barnaby St John Smythe was not entirely sure what it was he was asking.

'A diversion, sir.' Perkins pulled his cell phone from his pocket and dialled a number.

Lord Coe felt his cell phone vibrate and looked at the message screen. It was no-one he knew but in the light of the events he, along with tens of thousands of others, was witnessing it was best if he was one step ahead of the pack. He had a presentiment that the phone call was connected to these events. Was it going to be a blackmail? Extortion? The demand for some form of pay off?

'Lord Coe?' said the smooth, educated voice. 'You don't know me but my name is Perkins.'

Perkins? Why was he giving his name? Obviously, it must be a false name.

'Yes, Mr Perkins?' Lord Coe spoke warily, talking over his own interior monologue. 'And what can I do for you?'

'It's about the torch.'

'Yes, I thought it might be.' What outrageous demand were they about to make? It didn't matter. His own reputation for putting on a trouble free Olympics was in ruins. It didn't matter how much work he had put in. It didn't matter how much they had got right: the stadiums, the arrangements, the distribution of tickets, the strict accountancy provisions. None of that mattered. He had tripped on the last bend. He would not be sprinting now towards glory and further honours. It was over. Some of this must have flavoured his words.

'Lord Coe. The true flame is on its way.'

True flame? What was he talking about?

'Lord Coe. Please listen to me and listen carefully. The torch that exploded on Millennium Bridge was not the true flame. It's a long story and I'll tell you what happened another time. However, I have made arrangements for the true flame to be with you in ten minutes. The opening ceremony can start on time. But ...'

Despite himself, his heart had given a might jump for joy. All was not lost. This man Perkins seemed to know what he was talking about and so far he hadn't mentioned money. Not yet anyway. Maybe that was still to come, in some last second final twist to the plot. And there was a last twist. There was this dangling 'but' for a start. What was this 'but' about?

'Please tell your security men to allow a man on a motorcycle carrying a well known French athlete on the pillion to enter the stadium. There, your chosen athlete will collect the torch and go and light the Olympic flame.'

'But how can I be sure that this is the true flame?'

'Let's deal with that another time. If your researches are that the flame is not the true flame you can make all the necessary arrangements for relighting the torch. But I do assure you this is the true flame and it will save the day. The motor cycle should now be close to St Paul's. Please make sure the police are alerted to let it through, and also the little white van a hundred or so yards behind it. That's where I will be. We can discuss everything when we get to the stadium.'

Lord Coe made the necessary phone calls.

❧

Catherine Zeta Jones had to interrupt her commentary when a security man standing behind her stepped forward and passed her his phone. She listened intently to what she was being told and then, God bless her, for she is an actress and therefore used to following directions, no matter how absurd and idiotic they might at first appear to be.

'I have just heard some exciting news,' she announced. 'The events we have just been witnessing have been staged as a diversion because there was a threat of a terrorist attack. However the perpetrators have now been apprehended and the true flame is now on its way.' On the screen the crowds saw the motorbike cruise down the centre of the crowd lined streets. On the back of the bike Marguerite waved the torch in celebration and the roar of the crowd carried them both forward. For each of them in their own particular way it felt like redemption, a joining of their individually isolated souls to the mighty soul of mankind itself. It felt like they were coming home and, surprisingly, it felt good.

And so the flame reached the stadium and was handed over to that athlete who had been given the honour of racing that last stretch of track to the brazier where the Olympic flame presides over the races and competitions. You have all seen it. I do not need to waste my time or yours by repeating it.

What was not widely reported was that, at about the same time as the lighting ceremony, there was an explosion. A small white van parked in a side street not far from the main procession suddenly erupted in flames and pieces of the van were hurled up to fifty metres away. Investigations showed that the van was empty at the time. One witness says he saw four or five men hurriedly leave the van a few minutes earlier. Fortunately, no-one was hurt in the incident. Police believe this may have been a prank associated with a betting syndicate who placed a rather large sum of money on the prediction that there would be just such an explosion. However, this explosion was too far away from the stadium to win the bet. According to the police, there appeared to be some connection between these betting syndicates and a central Asian country. No other details were available.

Part Six

The lighting of the Olympic flame was the moment the London Olympics exploded (if I can use this metaphor) into life. The great spectacles of dance and light and music erupted on to millions—what am I saying? On to hundreds of millions—of television screens all around the world. Once again the orgy of athletics, sport, gymnastics and all the other components that make the Olympics what they are was upon the world. And the world loved it. The world revelled in it. This was a squandering of wealth on a grand scale. Then, after the spectacles were over, the marches began: Afghanistan, Albania, Algeria, Andorra, Angola ... out they came, one after the other, their proud flags flying; their proud athletes marching. Barbados, Belarus, Belgium ... on and on. Lord Coe smiled a smile that gave little indication of the enormous sense of inward relief and contentment that he was feeling. He had in the end steered this great ship into port. It had been touch and go in the end, and he had had to rely on the help of strangers but nevertheless, when this thing was over and he had handed the various stadia on to their new long term owners, he would be able to look back in pride. Indeed he would be able to look at himself firmly in the mirror and say to himself. Well done, Seb, you old son. You did it. Yes, he would be able to say that. And he would feel immensely proud of this achievement for the rest of his natural life.

There had of course been a long delay while he had discussed events with Perkins. It had taken a while for his cynicism to give way to simple incredulity and then to sheer, open-mouthed, stunned admiration. Perkins had contacted the whole team and Lord Coe had met them, shaken their hands and thanked them. Who would have thought that little runt Rowan Jones could have been such an effective motivator of men. Wonders would never cease. It was clear something had to be done to help these men and women who had saved the day. In particular he had been moved by the tears of that strange creature who called herself Anna but who clearly would have problems satisfying the requirements of femaleness, which in the world of the Olympics had a very special meaning. He had noticed she was crying and had done what he could to cheer her up.

'You are not happy?' he had asked.

'Oh I am! I am!' she assured him.

'Why are you crying?'

'Because I am so happy and because I am so sad, all at the same time.' The extremely expensive mascara streaked her cheeks. 'Because now there is nothing to stop the Olympics from going ahead. And because ...' she had waved her hands in voiceless distress, 'because I am no longer a man. But I am not quite a woman. I am a freak. I am an in-between thing that doesn't exist, for which there is no name. I am a nothing.'

'And yet,' Lord Coe had attempted to support her. 'Without you, President Osmanakhian would have succeeded in his terrible plan to explode a bomb. So you are a hero, a heroine.'

She had not been mollified and Lord Coe understood the reason. Then he had an idea. It would require an emergency session of the International Olympic Committee. He called an assistant to set up the meeting immediately.

219

And then there had been the near impossible task of ousting President Osmanakhian. He could still hear that awful man's strident voice.

'Hang him!' he had screamed, pointing his gloved hand at Lord Coe. 'Torture him! Throw him into the dungeons!' Lord Coe chuckled it had been quite a performance.

'You can't arrest me! I've got diplomatic immunity!' Osmanakhian quivered and slithered, coiling and uncoiling in rapid succession. But there was no escape. The line of evidence had been clear and thoroughly incriminating. The man had to be expelled. The more public the humiliation the better. And to top it off there were rumours of unrest in Transcaucasia. Perhaps by the time his plane landed he would have been overthrown. Lord Coe sincerely hoped so. Let him taste the dungeons for himself. Let him savour that experience. Lord Coe chuckled at the thought.

❦

Osmanakhian had been taken straight to nearby London city airport and put on his own plane. Within forty-five minutes the silver fuselage of Transcaucasia One was hurtling down the runway and then up and away into the light blue of the late afternoon sky. Freddy Fruhmanhoff caught sight of it as it arced in the air over Kingston, the sunlight glinting off it. He had only just emerged from the house having been kept awake all night by the most fiendish howling coming from the heart of the maze. He really must sell up. The lawn was against him, now too was the maze. Maybe he would be better off on the other side of the Atlantic. And in the plane President Osmanakhian snarled at his companions, Major Pavlov, Captain Polinka, two white haired scientists whose names he'd long since forgotten and whose future hung in the most delicate balance. And of course there was the Precious Ornament with the little dog on her lap. It was yapping fretfully, aware through doggy means that all was not as it should be. Osmanakhian picked it up and hurled it down the aisle. 'Bloody dog!' he growled. And then below them was the sea of the English Channel. They were on their way home.

❧

Eritrea, Estonia, Ethiopia … on came the marching athletes carrying their flags. On and on it went. The joy being in the multitudes, the weight of sheer numbers. Black skins, brown skins, yellow skins, pink skins. The numbers and the varieties. Tall, short, thin, stocky. Jamaica, Japan, Jordan, Kazakhstan … The sound of anthem upon anthem. He was mesmerized, enthralled, as was everyone in the stadium and all those in the streets of London and elsewhere throughout Britain who were watching these events on the screens that had been set up. And of course too there were all those at home with their slippers and cups of cocoa. What a celebration! Fireworks were still popping in the darkening sky, the golden flowers blossoming and then collapsing, fluttering down over the city, this mighty metropolis. Macedonia, Madagascar, Malawi, Malaysia …

'This is magnificent,' Lord Haverford, sitting beside him, commented. 'You must be very proud.'

Lord Coe turned to him and nodded his thanks.

'Yes, I am.' He said simply, for that was the simple truth.

'I'm so sorry Anna has missed this. Where has she got to?' He looked around again in that bewildered way he had that gave a glimpse of the boy at the core of the man. He would have gone in search of her if he had known where to look but each time he had half risen in his chair Lord Coe had patted his arm.

'I'm sure she knows what she's doing. She'll turn up.'

'I do hope so,' he muttered and one could sense in the awful deep melancholy of the words the incipient desolation should she fail to do so. How quickly she had curled up in the cosy nook of his heart.

And now finally they were coming to the end. Venezuela, Vietnam, Yemen, Zambia, Zimbabwe ... and after Zimbabwe there was another flag and still more athletes. What country came after Zimbabwe? He racked his brains but nothing came. It was then that Lord Haverford heard the voice of the announcer.

'And finally, bringing up the rear, we have those athletes who are running under the flag of the Olympic Association itself. Let me remind you that these are athletes who for whatever reason do not have a country to represent or who do not wish to represent their country ....'

Lord Haverford gazed down on the motley group of men and women. How Anna would have loved to be there. Where was the girl? And then, with a start, Lord Haverford realized he recognized some of the athletes and then others. There was Leonardo of course. Now that the cameras had zeroed in on him there were gasps and moans from several sections of the stadium. A woman nearby screamed: 'I love you!' and fainted. Berl's Babes were all dancing up and down and shrieking that ecstatic shriek more normally associated with thirteen year old girls and the Beatles. And then he saw Marguerite, tall and imperiously arrogant. And there was little Jade and Mad Mike and Ayesha—and Ayesha had her arms round the shoulders of Karl and Leona. And wasn't Leona looking ecstatic too—as if she'd already won gold or more. And oh my God! The entire Welsh basketball team and Jeremiah and the Japanese twins Yoshi and Toshi. And there was Ivan in the middle of the huddle of Tibetan Buddhist monks. Oh Anna! You are missing this! Where are you? And Kono had his arm wrapped languidly round Solomon's shoulders. Anna! What are you missing? And there was Barnaby and Perkins too of all people and Rowan Jones as well bringing up the rear, walking hand in hand with Bronwyn who was carrying a duck, and that wasn't a hat on her head but a cat!

And the voice of the announcer once again broke in over the sound of the cheers and screams of delight.

'These athletes are a symbol of the original Olympic charter which states very clearly that the goal of the Olympic movement is to contribute to the building of a peaceful and better world by educating youth through sport practiced without discrimination of any kind and in the Olympic spirit, which requires mutual understanding with a spirit of friendship, solidarity and fair play.' 'Oh Anna!' Lord Haverford sighed. 'Where are you? You are missing this most poignant of moments. You should be a witness to this.'

Lord Coe took out his opera glasses and handed them to Lord Haverford who stared at them uncomprehending.

'Take a look at the flag bearer.' Lord Coe suggested gently.

Lord Haverford raised the glasses to his eye and swept them along the crowd until he found the group, then he caught sight of the flag. Slowly his focus descended until he found himself staring into Anna's shining face.

'So there you are my sweet,' Lord Haverford murmured. 'There you are!' But then waves of confusion unsettled his brow. 'But I don't understand. How can she? He? No dammit, definitely she. I mean ...?'

'You are asking,' Lord Coe paraphrased. 'How is it that Anna, being neither a man, nor properly a woman, can take part in the Games?'

'Yes,' Lord Haverford spluttered. 'That's the question. How ... how ... how?'

Lord Coe smiled.

'It was really very simple. We're just following the Olympic charter. Remember what the great man Baron de Coubertin said: there must be no discrimination of any kind.'

'But, but ...' Lord Haverford stuttered.

'I don't know why we didn't think of it earlier. But better late than never.'

'What on earth are you talking about?'

'Well, on the one hand we have the men in the men's competition and on the other side we have the women in the women's competition. All we did was to create a third category for people who are—how can I put this?—somewhere in the middle.'

'I say, old chap!' Lord Haverford was beaming from end to end. 'A stroke of genius.'

About the Author

Jonathan Chamberlain is the author of the *Cancer: The Complete Recovery Guide* Series in eight volumes:

1. **Cancer? What Now?**
   Make sure the first steps of your cancer journey are heading in the right direction

2. **Cancer: Diagnosis and Conventional Treatments.**
   The Pros and Cons of Cancer Tests, Surgery, Radiation and Chemotherapy

3. **Cancer: Research and Politics**

4. **Cancer: Detox and Diet**

5. **Cancer: Herbs, Botanicals and Biological Therapies**

6. **Cancer: Vitamins and Other Supplements**

7. **Cancer: Energy, Mind and Emotions**

8. **Cancer: Survivors' Stories: They did it. You can too!**

He has also written two other books on cancer:
   Cancer: The Complete Recovery Guide (2008 edition)
   Cancer Recovery Guide: 15 Alternative and Complementary Strategies for Restoring Health

In addition he has two cancer-related websites at:
   www.fightingcancer.com and
   www.cancerfighter.wordpress.com

Jonathan has written a number of other works of fiction and non-fiction (see www.blacksmithbooks.com) and has founded two charities for families of children with developmental disabilities: the Hong Kong Down Syndrome Association, and Mental Handicap Network China.

Lightning Source UK Ltd.
Milton Keynes UK
UKOW022119291211

184469UK00004B/2/P